"Do you want to stay the night?"

"I'd like nothing more," Slade admitted. "But you have to know—"

Melinda put her fingers over his lips to stop the words that would have warned her about him and his family.

"No more talking," she said. "We both know the facts, but tonight is for us. Just you and me...and our new child."

He wrapped his arm around her waist and lifted her off her feet and carried her toward the stairs that led to her bedroom.

After this day, which had felt like a lifetime, he needed this. Needed her in a way that he never would want to admit to another soul. But she did something to him that went beyond sex.

He wanted to take her in the hallway up against the wall. Just take her hard and deep until there was no doubt that she was his.

No matter what logic said, his instincts demanded he make Melinda *his*.

* * *

Texas-Sized Scandal is part of the
Texas Cattleman's Club: Houston series.

Dear Reader,

I love Texas! Any opportunity I get to write another book about the Texas Cattleman's Club, I jump at. And this story was so juicy and fun to write. Melinda Perry is a good girl and, honestly, a really sweet woman. For me, she was so relatable. I'm one of those people who follows all the rules and expects—no matter how delusional it makes me sound—that everything in life will be fair. I had an attorney tell me one time that wasn't realistic, but it should be. ;)

Slade Bartelli lives by his own set of rules, too. He's a good man with a bad reputation that he has struggled his entire life to overcome. He's been pretty good at sticking to his own rules until he meets Melinda. She's different—while she's sweet and funny, she's also sexy as hell and not afraid to take what she wants. She just does it in her own way.

These characters both resonated a lot with me. Slade is Italian American, as am I, and there are certain things about his family that I might have borrowed from my own. It's just fun to add in how connected to everyone you are when you're Italian American. No matter what it is I need done, I have a cousin who does it. I'm not even kidding!

I hope you enjoy this latest installment in the Texas Cattleman's Club: Houston miniseries.

Happy reading!

Katherine

KATHERINE GARBERA

—

TEXAS-SIZED SCANDAL

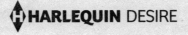

HARLEQUIN DESIRE

Special thanks and acknowledgment are given
to Katherine Garbera for her contribution to the
Texas Cattleman's Club: Houston miniseries.

PLEASE RECYCLE · THIS PRODUCT IS RECYCLABLE

ISBN-13: 978-1-335-60385-2

Recycling programs
for this product may
not exist in your area.

Texas-Sized Scandal

Printed in U.S.A.

HARLEQUIN®
™ www.Harlequin.com

Books by Katherine Garbera

Harlequin Desire

The Wild Caruthers Bachelors

Tycoon Cowboy's Baby Surprise
The Tycoon's Fiancée Deal
Craving His Best Friend's Ex

Cole's Hill Bachelors

Rancher Untamed

This book is dedicated to Lenora Worth,
Julia Justiss and Eve Gaddy, my soul sisters.
Thanks for always listening and having my back
and giving me a safe place to share the ugly bits
of life and then helping me to see the silver lining.

Prologue

Sterling Perry has to be feeling pretty smug now that he has been released from jail on fraud charges. Damn. The evidence should have been enough to keep him in jail. Nothing is going as planned. Ever since Vincent— Well, that doesn't matter. No one has any idea who killed the man. I guess I'll just have to direct them toward a suspect.

Perry is the most logical choice. The hatred the thought of him stirs inside me makes me want to punch someone. But instead I just take a deep breath and fight to find the calm part of myself. The part that makes it easier for me to plot the demise of the men who have stolen everything from me.

It's not as if they are good men. They both have flaws, too many to name, and they've hurt many people along the way. Collateral damage like me. But not anymore.

Ryder Currin and Sterling Perry are doing a good job of torturing each other, which doesn't hurt the plans that have been put in motion. But it wouldn't hurt to get Sheriff Battle on the case. He's a bulldog and would help to add fire to the charges simmering around Sterling Perry.

That text was sent from Vincent on a Perry Holdings phone. Everyone knows that no one does anything at Perry Holdings without Sterling's approval. That should be enough to get the case focused back on Sterling.

Glancing down at the email that has just arrived, a feeling of self-satisfaction spreads throughout me. Ryder Currin has some employment issues. Interesting. It shouldn't be that hard to get the information into Sterling Perry's hands and then let him use his information to ruin Currin.

It's hard not to feel self-satisfied. So embezzling didn't work out. There are still a couple of irons in this fire. Both of them are going to pay for what they've done. No matter how long it takes.

One

Melinda Perry glanced at her phone as she put the last hot roller in her hair. She was trying to ween herself off her social media addiction. While she loved knowing exactly what her faves were doing, she had learned she functioned better with far less FOMO if she started her day with a mug of... She wanted to say hot lemon water, but she'd never been able to make herself acquire a taste for it. No matter how unhealthy it was, she always started her day with coffee, a teaspoon of hot cocoa mix and non-fat half-and-half.

She glanced at the clock on her vanity mirror; she was running ahead of schedule. "Okay, Jeeves, give me the latest society news from the *Houston Chronicle*," she said. She'd programmed her electronic assistant to answer to Jeeves because she thought it was funny to pretend she had a proper British butler and because it had been going off whenever the commercial for it had come on prior to that.

"Good morning, Mels. Here's today's headline—'Heiress and philanthropist Melinda Perry is going hot and heavy with notorious playboy Slade Bartelli. Photos available on *Houston Chronicle* dot com.'"

"Okay, Jeeves, stop," she said, fumbling for her phone and opening the *Houston Chronicle* app. *Oh, no.* She didn't want to be on the society pages. She didn't want the world to know about her love affair with Slade.

Her family had been a hot mess for the last year and she had struggled to remain above it. Going about her business and acting as if everything were okay. Her father had been accused of running a Ponzi scheme, arrested and released from jail. Her sister was having a scandalous relationship with one of her father's most hated business rivals. And of course, she had started a romance with the son of notorious mobster Carlo Bartelli.

To be fair, Slade wasn't part of his father's crime syndicate and she had met him at a charitable committee meeting. He was an upstanding citizen but the media never seemed to care about that.

As soon as she opened the app, she saw a photo

of herself and Slade embracing…okay, kissing. Hot and heavy kissing in one of the alcoves of the Houston Symphony at Jones Hall.

She felt panic rise inside of her and her pulse raced. She was hot and bothered not only from being exposed but from remembering that kiss. She had to end this. It was getting out of control. She was behaving in a way that didn't suit her at all. Sure, she was thirty-nine and, as her twin had pointed out, not getting any younger.

If not now, then when? That's what Angela had said when Melinda had shyly mentioned she was seeing someone different from her usual type of guy.

But this wasn't what Melinda had had in mind. She liked her charity work, her quiet life. Also, Angela had been very plain in her disapproval of Slade as a lover for Melinda. Not that she needed her twin's approval of the man she dated.

She heard the sound of Pixie, her miniature dachshund, barking and then her bedroom door opened and her sister Angela walked into the room. They lived in the same building and always nipped into each other's places. The design of the condo was an open concept on the main living level and then an upper-level loft that was the master bedroom, bathroom and a living/sitting room that Melinda used as a workout space.

"I thought you weren't sure that Slade was the

right man for you. Didn't you say you wanted to be a mom? He's a legendary playboy, you know that, right?"

"No need to ask how you found out," she said. "I just didn't know if we were serious or not and I didn't want to make a big deal."

"That photo looked pretty serious to me," Angela said. She sat down on the tufted bench at the end of Melinda's bed.

Her sister had a thermal mug in her hand and looked fashionable as always. No matter how hard Melinda tried, she always felt like the serious, preppy twin. She knew that no one else would ever call her that, but she was the quieter twin, in fashion and in personality. If anyone should have been dating Slade, it was Angela.

"That picture... I had no idea anyone would see us, or I never would have kissed him like that," Melinda admitted.

"You're blushing! We're thirty-nine, Mels. It's time for you to stop blushing when you talk about sex."

"I wasn't talking about sex! Slade just makes me hot. It's not embarrassment, it's— Oh, never mind. What am I going to do?" she asked her sister.

"Do you like him?" Angela asked.

Like him?

She hadn't thought about it that way. He was so intense. She knew about his family's rumored mob connections, but when she was with him, he focused on her. He made her feel…like she was the only woman in the world. And the most passionate person he'd ever met. But honestly, she knew that was only because of him. Donald, her ex-boyfriend of eight years, always complained that she hadn't brought any va-va-voom, but with Slade that wasn't an issue.

"I know you don't approve of him. You've made that very clear and I'm not sure how I feel about him. He's on the art council, which is how we met."

"He's on the art council? I thought his family were all mobsters—which, by the way, concerns me."

"He's not a mobster, Angela. He is also the only grandson of Philomena Conti. So he's representing the family. I think Mrs. Conti had a hip replacement earlier this year, which is why he filled in at the meeting. We just hit it off. He likes art as much as I do. It was my description of a Van Dyck that made him notice me."

Angela stood up and walked over to her, putting her hands on Melinda's shoulders and making her face the mirror. She met her sister's gaze, avoiding looking at herself. She had the big rollers in because it made doing her hair easier, and she hadn't put on any makeup yet so her freckles were visible.

"Look at yourself," Angela said.

She glanced up at her own reflection. She always

smiled at herself because that helped her start the day in a good mood. Angela smiled back at her as well.

"That man noticed you because of you," she said. "And it's about time that you found a man who can make you forget yourself at the opera."

Melinda sighed. She knew her sister was right. No matter what Slade made her feel, at the end of the day their lives simply didn't fit together. He was more Cristal champagne and parties at his penthouse and jetting off to Dubai than local artist openings.

"I know. Not the danger part—he's really not a bad man, Angela. But he's not for me either. Honestly, I sort of thought after we slept together, he'd move on to someone else," Melinda said. "But he hasn't. There's something between us that makes it hard to keep our hands off each other."

"Passion, Mels. Finally, you've found a guy who brings out the fire in you," Angela said. "But not a Bartelli. Find someone else."

Melinda shook her head. She didn't want the fire… Well, not all the time. Fire was dangerous. She knew that had led to trouble in her parents' relationship and she'd always striven to keep her life on an even keel.

But now she wasn't on an even keel. She was already really overdue for her period and she'd always been regular. Maybe she was having perimenopause. She had read an article that some women started to experience symptoms at her age.

She met her sister's eyes in the mirror and knew better than to bring up that subject again unless she'd taken a pregnancy test. As close as she and Angela were, there were some things that they both just kept to themselves and this was going to be one of them.

"If it were that easy, I would have done it a long time ago," she said at last. "I'm not sure where things are going with Slade, but we both know it's not going to last."

"Good," Angela said, giving her a breezy one-armed hug. "Are you okay?"

She wanted to nod but the hot rollers made her head feel heavy and awkward. "Of course. I'm always okay."

"Except I know that you're not. You said you wanted to be a mom…and suspected you were pregnant. Are you? Is he the father?" Angela asked.

She wasn't ready to talk about pregnancy. She hadn't even been to her doctor yet, even though she had bought more than a few over-the-counter tests. She hadn't gotten up the courage to take them yet. She might want to be a mom, but she had in her mind the way it should happen. She was a traditional kind of gal. She wanted Slade to fall in love with her—desperately in love—and propose marriage, to have a huge society wedding—where her father, sister and family weren't in the midst of a scandal—and then have a baby.

"I don't know if I'm pregnant," she said, dropping her gaze from Angela's in the mirror. She wasn't a big fan of lying to anyone, but she wasn't ready to deal with being pregnant while the *Chronicle* was running a photo of her and Slade kissing. "I mean, Slade Bartelli doesn't sound like the right kind of man for me, does he?"

Angela propped her hip on the edge of the vanity and looked pensively at Melinda's bedroom. For the first time, Melinda realized that her sister might be hiding something of her own. "Are you okay? How are your wedding plans coming along?" Angela had just announced her engagement to Ryder Currin.

"Yeah, I'm fine. Nice try, but we are talking about you," Angela said. "I don't know what to tell you. If you say Slade's a good guy… Well, I'm on your side. Just make sure you know what you're doing. While fire is good and I have always thought that's what you needed to shake you out of your routines and lists, it can also burn you. I don't want to see you hurt."

Melinda turned and hugged her sister, resting her head against her stomach. "I don't want you hurt either. Men are…way more complicated than they look on the surface."

Her sister laughed as she started taking out the

hot rollers in Melinda's hair. "They are. Why can't they just be hot, right?"

"Yes. And sophisticated and like the things we like and then go away when we need to get back to real life."

Her sister laughed again. "If only we were in charge of the world."

"Someday," she said.

"Someday," Angela repeated quietly.

Angela left a few minutes later and Pixie came trotting into the room and plopped herself on her bed. Melinda leaned into the mirror to finish putting on her makeup and fixing her hair and then she got dressed for the day.

She took extra care to make sure her A-line skirt was straight, and her blouse tucked in properly; she didn't like it when it was too loose around the waist. She tied the pussy bow at the neckline and then switched the contents of her handbag to the purse that perfectly matched her magenta skirt. She had a lot of work to do at her foundation and meetings this morning.

She put her sunglasses on the top of her head, patted Pixie's head as she walked out the front door, then took the elevator down to the lobby of her building. Downstairs, she was met by a barrage of flashbulbs.

Panicked, she ducked back onto the elevator. She went back to her condo, texted her assistant she'd be out this morning and then hit the treadmill. Walking always helped her figure things out. Things were definitely getting too complicated and now she knew she had to end things with Slade. No one had ever noticed when she kissed Donald.

Slade Bartelli tossed his phone on the passenger seat of his Ferrari Lusso as he backed out of his parking space at his downtown offices. He'd been trying to get in touch with Melinda since he'd gotten the news notification from the *Houston Chronicle*. And nothing. Total radio silence.

She wasn't a fan of too much PDA, which he admitted was cute and one of the reasons why he liked her. She dressed like a lady but kissed like…well, like his hottest, wettest dreams. She was different, and he liked that about her. But his gut—the same one that had always warned him when trouble was at the door during his childhood—was telling him that if he didn't talk to her, she was going to walk out of his life without a backward glance.

Part of him—the part that he was constantly fighting with—wanted to find the paparazzo who'd taken that photo and pound him. But he wasn't that kind of Bartelli. He was trying to be the man his nonna Conti had raised him to be. But there were times when he had to admit his dad's way was a lot more efficient.

He pulled up in front of Melinda's building,

parking illegally out front because he knew the doorman would relish the chance to drive the Ferrari if the traffic cop came by. He saw the paparazzi as soon as he neared the building. They were snapping photos, calling his name, and he faced them with a snarl, ready to unleash hell or his version of it on them, until he heard the doorman calling his name.

Not Slade but Mr. Bartelli.

That's right. He was better than his mobster blood. But, he reminded himself, that didn't mean he was good enough for Melinda Perry. Despite the scandal that swirled around her family—he'd heard rumors that her father was implicated in a murder now—Melinda was always above it. She loved her family but she kept her distance. No one who looked at her would ever believe she was anything but good and kind. Things no one would ever say about him.

No matter that he had to remind himself of that several times a day.

"Johnny," he said, walking over to the doorman. "I'm here to see Ms. Perry. How long have they been here?"

"All day. I helped her sneak back onto the elevator. But they're persistent and won't leave."

"Have you called the cops?"

"Ms. Perry didn't want to. She said they're just doing their jobs."

Of course she did. She had a kind heart. "Let's get rid of them. I'll call the commissioner and take care of it. Also, will you keep an eye on my car? Move it if you need to."

"Yes, sir, Mr. Bartelli."

Slade walked into the lobby of Melinda's building and stood there for a moment, battling both sides of himself before he dialed his assistant and asked him to take care of the paparazzi.

"Yes, sir. Also, you had a call from your father. Not an emergency. He just wants to speak to you. And your grandmother expects you for dinner with Ms. Perry."

"Ignore my father. I'll take care of Nonna."

"Yes, sir."

He hung up with his assistant and immediately went to the elevator that led to Melinda's condo. He knew why everyone was interested in them as a couple. Because he was flashy and courted the media. It was the only way he knew to prove that he was aboveboard ever since he'd taken over running Conti Imports. He'd been under so much scrutiny that he'd hired a PR firm that had advised him to make sure everything he did was very public and had as much publicity as he could throw at it.

He'd never have guessed he'd like the attention as much as he did, but it suited him. He liked talking to the press; he didn't even mind it when they followed him around. But with Melinda, he knew that was just another mark against him. His dad was a rumored mob boss and Slade knew the old man had tried going clean a long time ago and he'd never been able to. That was another reason why Slade really liked working for his mom's side of the family.

His dad had one time said that once he took his job as a hit man, there was no turning back. And Slade never wanted to be on that path. As much as his gut always wanted him to take the easy way, he fought it and made sure he never did.

But Melinda messed up his gut. She had him so hot and horny he felt like he was eighteen and not almost forty. He hadn't been this turned on by a woman in a long time. But it was more than the sex that was fabulous. It was the way she poured herself into her passions like art and opera.

When he got off the elevator on the twenty-fourth floor and walked toward her condo, he hesitated. It would be better for her if he let her drift out of his life. He knew that media attention wasn't something she was going to enjoy. And he'd done a good job of keeping their relationship private. Until now, obviously. He had to admit that he'd done it not for her—well, not consciously for her—but more for himself. So much of his life was in the spotlight that it had been nice to have someone who was just his. No one knew about her, and he knew she liked it that way as well. Though she might say that his family name didn't matter to her, he knew it did.

Hell, he wasn't even sure that Nonna was going to approve of him and Melinda. And of all the people on the planet, she was the one who loved him the most and always thought he deserved the best.

He pushed the doorbell and heard Pixie barking in the condo, but there was no answer. He waited for a few minutes and then punched the doorbell again.

Pixie didn't bark this time, which made him suspect that Melinda was in there and didn't want to talk to him. He knocked on her door one last time. "It's me. Slade. Let me in, so we can sort this out."

He waited, not sure if she would open the door for him, and another minute passed before she finally did and he saw her standing there. Her long blond hair was pulled back in a high ponytail—the kind she favored—that accentuated her heart-shaped face. Her blue eyes were troubled, and she'd chewed off all the lipstick he was sure she'd put on that morning. She had on her workout gear, which showed off her athletic physique. Her skin appeared pale and she didn't smile when she saw him, which set warning bells off in his mind.

Melinda smiled at everyone. *Everyone.* The bellhop who opened her door, the barista who made her coffee, the doorman. She was one of the friendliest people he'd ever met. Now, though, she didn't step back to invite him inside.

"Are you okay?" he asked. He had no idea how to fix this. To be honest, he knew that she had liked their low-key relationship but this reaction… Was she embarrassed by him?

"I've had better days, but yes, I'm fine," she said, clearly lying to him as she had one arm wrapped around her stomach as if she were trying to hold herself together.

"I don't know how the media were alerted to our presence at the opera last night. I know my people didn't say anything," he said. "I've got a call into the police department to get rid of the paparazzi who are hanging out downstairs. We'll get on top of this and get it sorted out."

"Will we?" she asked. "Why?"

"Why? I thought we liked hanging out together," he said. "Isn't that reason enough? Why don't you let me come in and we can talk about it?"

She shook her head. "If you come in, we will probably do more than talk and I need to be clear-headed about this, Slade."

He smiled at the way she said it. "You are being clearheaded. I promise to be on my best behavior."

Melinda's building was sleek and modern, a tall high-rise made of glass and steel, but her condo was much like the woman herself, warm and welcoming. The entryway had an antique hall tree, on which she always kept a vase with fresh-cut flowers in it. Moving into the main open living space, he noted the two large couches as well as two armchairs, all in cordovan leather that he knew from experience were buttery soft and the most comfortable chairs he'd ever sat in.

Her coffee table was made of reclaimed wood, where she kept art books on her latest obsession. Right now, he knew she was researching Dalí for an exhibit the art council wanted to bring to Houston. But she also had a few magazines that she kept tucked in a basket on the lower shelf of the table. She'd even started storing the business magazines he liked to read there.

Her kitchen was demarked by a tall countertop with high-back stools. The cushions matched the colors of the large Cruz Ortiz painting that hung above her fireplace. The colors of the Ortiz painting were bright and reflected, in Melinda's words, the *vibrancy of Texas*.

She stood there between the living room and the kitchen, watching him with her eyes wide and troubled. He had done this to her. It hadn't been his intent, but he was bringing scandal to her door the way her father and her sister had. Something he'd promised himself he wouldn't do.

"I like it when you're at your best," she said, then shook her head. "See? No. You can't come in. I'm not me when you're around."

He didn't like the way she said that. As if he were a bad influence on her. "I think you're more yourself with me than you've ever been before."

Two

Melinda wished she'd left the door closed, but manners had forced her to open it and now the plan she'd hatched to break up with Slade and get back to her normal life wasn't going to be easy at all. He stood there, looking so hot, his square jaw with a little bit of stubble, his thick black hair curled a little on the top and his lips firm. And oh, her stars, she really wanted nothing more than to blurt out everything that had happened since Angela had left that morning. But she hadn't yet decided what she was going to do about anything.

"I'm actually glad you stopped by," she said. "Can I get you something to drink? Maybe some sweet tea or lemonade?"

"I'm fine. I'm more concerned that you haven't returned my texts or calls. What's up?"

"Oh, well, are you sure you don't want something to drink? Even water?" she asked. She was stalling and though she normally prided herself on being brave and facing difficult situations, she was going to give herself a pass today. She really had more than one woman should have to deal with. An image of the seven—SEVEN—pregnancy tests she'd taken lined up on her bathroom counter flashed into her mind.

"I'm positive," he said. "What's going on, babe? I know you don't like the media spotlight, but it was one kiss and, honestly, the photo isn't that bad. Are you concerned that you might be linked to the rumors about your father? I know I'm probably the last man you want by your side while murder rumors are swirling."

The murder victim had been found at the Texas Cattleman's Club newest site in Houston, at her father's Perry Construction site, and the victim was Vincent Hamm, a Perry Holdings employee, and her father was on the short list of suspects.

She shrugged, searching for the words. She couldn't just blurt out that she liked to rise above scandal. That she expected more of herself and her family or that she didn't like for anyone to see her looking so...well, totally enthralled by him. Slade gave off that aura of danger and that was part of what drew her to him, but the truth was she didn't want the world—rather, her world, the Houston society circle she traveled in—to see that embrace and judge her.

"It's a lot of things. Frankly, I think we both know we aren't right for each other," she said. "I figured I was a novelty for you, and you'd get bored and break up with me before this."

"Yeah, well, I'm not bored. Are you?" he asked. His tone was almost belligerent, but she could sense the vulnerability beneath it.

She'd learned that being Carlo Bartelli's son brought with it a lot of expectation of the kind of man Slade was. And he spent a lot of his time pretending not to be upset by being prejudged by his last name.

She chewed her lower lip before she realized what she was doing. She'd never be bored with Slade. He was exciting and everything that she'd always dreamed of finding in a man. But dreams weren't reality and she knew that better than most. She'd always wanted a picture-perfect family and hers was far from that.

"No, I'm not bored, but we really aren't cut out to be a couple. I mean, when I saw that photo I blushed remembering everything that followed. But you... What did you do?"

He came closer to her and she stepped back, which made him pause. She wasn't normally someone who backed down from anything, but honestly, she wasn't prepared to be in the middle of this kind of mess. It was one thing to stand on the sidelines and offer advice to Angela or sympathy to her father, but to have the papers talking about her? That wasn't in her plan. But heck, when had anything gone according to plan since Slade had come into her life?

"Are you afraid of me?"

"No, never," she admitted. "It's me. I have no self-control around you, Slade."

"From my point of view, that's a good thing," he said with that wicked smile of his that made her remember all the reasons why she'd kissed him at the opera the night before.

She felt the blush creeping up her neck and cheeks and shook her head. She wished she could stop doing that, but she'd never been able to control it. "That's exactly what I'm talking about. The reason why we need to break up. I mean, is that too high school for us?"

"No," he said.

"No?" Which part was he saying *no* to? Did he think they should stop seeing each other? Or that the term *breakup* wasn't too high school? Why did she do that? She always asked complex questions because her mind was constantly running with a million thoughts.

"Both. We aren't breaking up and it's not too immature to say it. I'm not going to let one picture taken by some intruding paparazzo intrude on us."

She loved the way he sounded. So in control of

his life and never letting the outside dictate who they were. But at the same time, she knew that it wasn't that simple. At the end of the day, rumors still abounded about him being a mobster, even though he had reassured her he wasn't part of his father's illegal operations.

And now there was an even bigger reason she needed to walk away from Slade. She was pregnant. All those home test kits had proven her suspicions.

From now on, she had to make all of her choices based on that. Before, it was okay for her to pretend that Slade was going to turn out to be one of the white knights she read about in her books. But real life told her that a man who lived as large as he did would never be happy with her quiet life.

She knew that.

She had to remember that.

She couldn't be tempted by the way he offered her everything she'd ever wanted.

She had to think of her baby.

"What are you thinking?" he asked. "You're looking at me with both longing and fear, and I'm not sure what to make of that."

She took a deep breath. "I'm thinking that as exciting as it is dating you, I know that there is no future in this. I think we should stop seeing each other."

"No."

She shook her head, not sure she'd heard him properly. She smiled and tried again. "I mean you and I really are two different types of people and it makes more sense for us to stop going out."

"No," he said again.

She took another deep breath. Sometimes people didn't take her seriously because she was soft-spoken and polite, and they took her ladylike manners and modest dress to mean she was a pushover. But Slade should know better. The fact that he didn't just cemented in her mind that they definitely weren't meant to be.

And he was making her lose her temper.

"You can say no as much as you want, but at the end of the day, my decision is final. I'm not going to go out with you anymore. I'm not going to be on the society pages kissing you. I know it seemed to you as if I were asking you what you thought, but I wasn't. I'm telling you. This is over."

This was worse than he'd thought, but he'd faced tougher situations. For a moment, Slade thought about just leaving. It was the lady's request, but he wasn't entirely sure that she wanted him gone. He had been walking a tightrope with Melinda since they'd met in a committee meeting.

He remembered that afternoon vividly. She'd been dressed very prim and proper, yet she'd made some hilarious comments under her breath to him while the meeting had been going on. Then apologized later because she'd said she was used to his nonna getting her sense of humor. She'd been such a contradiction that he couldn't help but want to learn more about her. So, he'd asked her out.

She'd said no.

He'd asked her out again, claiming he needed her help because he was representing the Conti family, and she immediately said yes. One thing had led to another and they'd wound up in bed. He couldn't regret any of it.

And he wasn't ready for it to end. If he believed that she was asking him to leave her alone because it was what she wanted, he'd do it in a heartbeat. But a big part of him thought it was due to the photo in the paper. She didn't like the limelight. She left that to her twin, Angela, and just kept to her quiet philanthropic work.

Her family had been one scandal after another lately and he knew that Melinda had been trying to rise above it while being supportive of everyone. Her twin was engaged to her daddy's business rival—Ryder Currin of Currin Oil—a man rumored to have had an affair with her mother years ago.

He knew he had to handle this delicately and if when he was done trying to convince her to give him another chance she still wanted him out of her life, he'd leave.

"I don't think you can just dictate things in our relationship," he said. "That's not really fair, is it? Is it because I'm a Bartelli?"

"Slade, you know I don't hold your family's reputation against you. You've assured me you have no part in that criminal world and I believe you," she said.

"Thank you for that," he said. He was always having to prove he wasn't a thug to most of the people he met. And as much as he was using the details of his life to make himself seem not good enough for her, he knew she'd jump to defend him.

"You don't have to thank me for that," she said, reaching out to gently squeeze his forearm. "You're a good man. Don't let anyone tell you otherwise."

"I won't," he said, taking her hand in his and running his thumb along the back of her knuckles. She shivered delicately.

"Is it because your family doesn't like me?"

"Seriously, if they ever met you, I'm sure you'd have them eating out of your hand in no time," she said. "You can be very charming when you want to be." She pulled her hand away from his. "I see what you're doing."

"What am I doing?"

"Trying to point out that there are a lot of good reasons for us to keep dating. But, Slade, you haven't taken into consideration that we are at our core very different people. I'm single, but there is a part of me that is always hoping that whomever I date will turn into Mr. Right-for-Me. I want the whole shebang—husband, family, big house in the suburbs—and when I'm being honest with myself, I can't see you as that guy to give them to me," she said.

He couldn't argue with that. "I'm not ever having kids, you know that. I don't want a child of mine to have to grow up like I did in the shadow of my father's reputation."

He'd told her that on the first night they'd gone out. They had stayed up until the early hours of morning, talking about life and family and just everything. He had been honest with her because she was Melinda and she was different from the other women he'd hooked up with. For one thing, she was his age and she didn't seem to be a part of the hookup culture. He hadn't wanted to hurt her in the long run. He still didn't.

And when she framed her objection to their being a couple that way, it was hard for him to keep on with his plan to talk her into not dumping him.

"I get that. I know I'm not a family man," he said. "But I'm not ready to say goodbye, Melinda."

She tipped her head to the side, studying him for a long moment before she nodded. "I'm afraid if I don't end things now, I never will, and when you do walk away, I won't find the man I need who can give me what you are making me realize I want."

Her words just made this even harder. She wanted him to stay but to turn into the man she dreamed of. And if there had ever been a man who was made for Melinda, he was the polar opposite of that. He knew the gentlemanly thing to do would be to walk out that door and never see her again. She was too good, too honest for the likes of him. But as much as he wanted to believe he wasn't a Bartelli through and through, he knew he was.

And he wanted her for himself. All he'd have to do was pretend he'd reconsider, and she'd be his, but he wondered if he could live with himself if he did that. Nonna always said one white lie was all it took to start down the path to the gray area that his father operated in. One where crimes were framed in a way to make it seem as if there were no other option.

He had to find a way to convince her to give him another chance. Because he wasn't ready to let her go. Not yet.

Three

He knew that he needed to do something to win her back.

He had no regrets about the PDA at the opera the night before. He was never going to be able to keep his hands off her. She called to him like nothing else in his life ever had. It intrigued him and kept him coming back for more.

But she was still nibbling on her lower lip and looking over at him, her blue eyes full of regret, longing and resolve. That didn't bode well.

"I'm sorry about the press. I have my man on it and he's going to put a spin on it that's going to make this all seem like nothing but harmless fun," he said. "That's what you want, right?"

She blinked rapidly and shook her head. He tried to keep his mind on her emotional state, but she wore a pair of leggings that hugged her curves, revealing her belly button and midriff. His fingers tingled with the need to reach out and touch her, caress her.

When she was in his arms, none of the other stuff mattered. It didn't matter that he was the reason the social bloggers and society pages were following her. He was the scandal. Not Melinda. She had spent her entire life doing good deeds in her work as a philanthropist. He'd never met someone who always thought of others before themselves.

He did a lot of good work at Conti Enterprises but in his gut, he knew it was to prove he wasn't like his father. Somehow, he was pretty damn sure that tinged the good deeds.

Neither did his family name matter once he held her in his arms, nor the fact that they really were very different people. Only the attraction and the passion between them mattered. That and the fact that she liked walking on the wild side with him. He knew she wasn't used to dating a man like him. Sure, she'd dated wealthy bachelors but most of them had been doctors or lawyers. Not sons of dangerous gangsters.

Once again, he realized how much he hated that part of himself. He was constantly at war with that side of himself and it had cost him opportunities all of his life. He knew that one day it would cost him Melinda Perry as well.

But it wouldn't be today.

"Slade—"

"Don't. Don't do this. Give me a chance before you kick me to the curb," he said.

"I shouldn't…but I want to," she said, biting her lower lip again.

This time he groaned. He reached out and rubbed his thumb along her lower lip. She had the kind of mouth that always inspired wet dreams in him, even when he sat across the table from her at a charity meeting. He couldn't help it. She was so prim and proper when they were in public.

But in private…

She bit his thumb and then sucked it into her mouth. He put his hand on her waist—God, she was so soft—and then he drew her closer until her body was pressed against his. He ran one finger around the waistband of her leggings and then let his finger slowly move up her spine.

She shivered in his arms and arched her back, thrusting her pelvis against his. He rubbed his erection into the notch between her thighs as she parted her legs to accommodate his hard-on. She put one hand on his shoulder and tipped her head back. Their eyes met and he knew this would solve nothing.

He wanted to believe that a day spent burning up the sheets would make all their problems go away, but he knew it wouldn't. That this wasn't going to do anything but distract them for a little while.

And since he'd sort of gotten used to being a distraction for her while her father had been under suspicion of financial wrongdoing, it was a role he fell easily into. He liked it because this was the one time when it didn't matter that he was the son of a dangerous man—a reputed mobster who had a long list of crimes he was suspected of committing, though there had never been any witnesses to convict him.

Except Slade.

No. He wasn't going there now. He was holding this gorgeous woman in his arms, and he planned to distract them both from the real world and their problems.

Cupping her butt, he lifted her off her feet and she wrapped her legs around his waist as he brought his mouth down on hers. That sexy mouth of hers melted under his and she pushed her fingers through his hair, holding him to her as she angled her head to deepen the kiss.

Her tongue rubbed over his and he sucked it deeper into his mouth as he moved toward the kitchen counter. It wasn't ideal, but it was the closest flat surface and he couldn't wait one more second. He set her down on the counter and stood between her spread legs. She didn't scoot back, still kept her ankles locked together, holding him with a grip that he knew he could break. But why would he want to?

He had everything that he'd always wanted right here in his arms. The publicity was a road bump, but they'd get past it and move on. They'd figure this out, but not right now. Right now, he had other things to focus on. Like the feel of her hand roaming down the front of his pants, cupping him and stroking his erection while she kissed the side of his neck.

"You like that, don't you?" she asked, her voice deeper than normal. A husky tone that sent shivers down his spine and made it damn near impossible for him to talk.

"Yeah."

She laughed at the way he grunted the word but then he took the hem of her sports bra in his hands and lifted it up over her head, tossing it aside. Her breasts were full and her nipples pert from being aroused. He reached down and cupped both breasts, rubbing his thumbs over her areolae until she was arching her back, thrusting her breasts toward him.

"You like that?" he asked her.

She just ran her finger around the tip of his erection until he was about to melt into a puddle at her feet. "Yeah."

He loved this. Loved the way she turned sex into fun. It wasn't a game of power with Melinda; it was always something they shared. Both of them enjoying every minute of it and neither one trying to manipulate the other.

Leaning down, he kissed the side of her neck,

working his way lower. She smelled of her flowery perfume and the sweat from her workout, and it made him even harder. He loved that she always felt real to him. Not like she was trying to be someone else. Melinda was one of the few people he knew who was always just herself. She owned her life and that was a big turn-on.

He nibbled on her and held her at his mercy. Her nails dug into his shoulders and she leaned up, brushing against his chest. Her nipples were hard points—he glanced down to see them pushing against his chest. He shifted his shoulders, rubbing his chest over hers, and she leaned forward to bite his neck, her fingers going to his tie. She undid it and then moved slowly down the front of his shirt, undoing the buttons and pushing the fabric open until he had to let her go to get the shirt off.

He wore French cuffs because it was something that set him apart from his father, but right now he regretted it as he fumbled to get the cuff links off. Melinda brushed his fingers aside and took them off, putting them on the countertop behind her.

"I got you these, didn't I? I like them because they require a woman's touch," she said.

"Your touch...not any other woman's. Actually, every part of me requires your touch," he said.

She ran her finger down his chest, swirling her finger around his nipple before moving lower toward his belly button. "Every part? Not just this one?"

She reached below his belt and caressed his hard-on through the fabric of his pants.

"Every part," he said, but the words were raspy, and speech was quickly becoming harder for him. He just wanted to rip her clothes from her body and take her.

He always fought against his animal instincts with Melinda. He wanted to protect her from that darkness inside of him, yet she called to it. And sometimes her touch tamed it.

But not right now.

She enflamed him and it was only the sheer force of his will that kept him from acting like the animal he knew he was.

He slowly drew his hand down the side of her neck, taking his time to note all of the things about her that excited him. She had a scar on her upper arm that she admitted she'd gotten when she'd fallen out of her high school boyfriend's pick-up truck. He rubbed his finger over the crescent shape, watching goose bumps spread down her arm, and then her nipples tightened even more.

He ran his other hand down her shoulder blade to the line of her spine, slowly caressing her back. She rolled her back against his touch, her breasts brushing against his chest. Slowly he worked his way down her back, taking time to fondle the indentation of her waist and then moving lower until he reached the base of her spine.

He cupped her butt and drew her forward until he could rub his erection against the center of her. She dug her nails into his shoulders and arched against him as he palmed her buttocks. She moaned and rubbed herself against him.

He wrapped one arm around her waist and lifted her off the countertop. With the other hand, he shoved her leggings down. Once she realized what he was doing, she helped him, pushing the fabric down her legs until she was free. He stepped back and just looked at her, sitting naked on her kitchen counter and he almost came in his pants.

Her eyes drifted closed and he saw her chest expand as she inhaled. He reached up and cupped her breasts, running his fingers over her distended nipples. He loved the pink perkiness of them and the way they responded to his every touch. He rubbed his fingers back and forth over them until her head dropped back and her back arched. He needed to make every sexual experience they had top the last. With any other woman that might have been difficult, but not with Melinda.

"Slade, baby, do that again," she moaned as she tipped her head to the side, exposing her long neck. He couldn't resist leaning down to nip at it, sucking against the pulse that beat strongly there. Her hands fell to his shoulders, holding on to him for a brief moment, and then she moved her hands down his arms. He flexed his biceps, knowing how much that excited her.

No one had ever turned him on this quickly before. Somehow, she was a thirst that he couldn't quench and as much as he knew that made her dangerous, he couldn't resist her.

He liked that she couldn't resist him either. She arched against him as he leaned down and sucked one nipple into his mouth. He looked up at her, wanting to remember her like this—turned on, so full of need and want and knowing he was the only one who could satisfy her.

A few tendrils had escaped her ponytail, but he wanted to feel her hair against him, so he pulled the hair tie from it and she shook her head as her hair fell around her shoulders, curling just above her breasts. He buried his head in the soft strands and inhaled deeply.

He noticed her eyes were heavy lidded as her hips began moving against him. He felt himself straining against the zipper of his trousers and reached between them to pull the zipper down and free himself.

He fumbled in his pocket for the condom he had stuck in there before coming over. She took it from him and their eyes met. Something passed over her face and he started to ask her what it was, but then it was gone. She undid his belt and shoved his pants down his legs, along with his boxers. The elastic got caught on his erection and he stepped back to shove them down his legs, taking the condom from her and putting it on.

She looked like something from his hottest fantasies. There were moments when he wondered why it had taken him so long to find a woman like Melinda, but then he knew his younger self wouldn't have known how to handle her.

He leaned down and licked the valley between her breasts, imagining his erection sliding back and forth there. He bit carefully at her delicate skin, suckling at her so that he'd leave his mark.

"Enough foreplay. Take me, Slade," she said. "I need to forget everything except this for a little while."

Her words enflamed him because he wanted nothing more than to drive himself into her again and again. No woman had affected him the way she did. She seemed to accept him as the man he was. Son of a mobster and grandson of one of the richest, most prominent women in Houston. She seemed to understand that both parts of him made him the man he was.

She spread her thighs, leaning back on her elbows, beckoning him to her. He groaned at the sight of her. This was an image he hoped to carry in his mind for the rest of his days, even after this affair ended. He knew it would. He was poison to a good woman like Melinda, but not for the short term.

He stepped between her legs, cupped her buttocks and drew her closer to him. Rubbing the tip of his erection against her center, nestling it to the opening of her body. She shifted against him, wrapping her arms around his shoulders as he entered her. Just the smallest bit because he couldn't wait.

She reached between his legs and fondled his sac, cupping him in her hands, and he shuddered. "If you keep doing that, this is going to be a very short experience."

She squeezed him and sucked his lower lip into her mouth. "I don't mind."

He held her hips steady and entered her slowly until he was fully sheathed. Her eyes widened with each inch he gave her. She clutched at his hips as he started thrusting, holding him to her, eyes half-closed and her head tipped back.

He leaned down and caught one of her nipples in his teeth, scraping very gently. She started to tighten around him. Her hips moved faster, demanding more, but he kept the pace slow, steady. Wanting her to come before he did.

He suckled her nipple and rotated his hips to catch her pleasure point with each thrust and he felt her hands in his hair, clenching as she threw her head back and her climax ripped through her.

He varied his thrusts, finding a rhythm that would draw out the tension at the base of his spine.

Something that would make his time in her body, wrapped in her silky limbs, last forever.

She scraped her nails down his back, clutched his buttocks and drew him in. Sensation feathered down his spine, his blood roared in his ears and everything in his world centered on Melinda.

He called her name as he came, collapsing against her chest. Her arms held him, one hand moving up and down his back, until his breathing steadied, and he shifted until he stood between her legs again. He looked down at her face and kissed her softly. He had no idea what he was going to do with Melinda. She wasn't the right woman for him, but he couldn't walk away.

He heard her doorbell ring and she looked at the two of them, still joined and naked.

"Who could that be?" she asked.

"I don't know," he answered. "Want me to handle it for you?"

She glanced at him as he stepped back and pulled on his trousers. "No. I need to do this. Let's go and get dressed and I'll take care of it."

She picked up her phone from the table and glanced at the video app to see who was there. "It's my sister Esme."

He lifted her off the counter, caressing her as he did so, and she batted his hands away. "Not now."

"Give me a minute," she yelled at the closed front door as she dashed upstairs to her bedroom. He collected their clothes and followed her upstairs to her bedroom. When he entered, she was already twisting her hair back into a ponytail and wearing a flowery patterned wraparound dress that accentuated her curves.

"Hurry back," he said as she kissed him before running out of the room. He couldn't last long without her.

Four

Melinda dealt with her younger sister as quickly as she could. Esme had just stopped by to make sure she was okay after hearing she hadn't gone to work, but honestly, she wasn't. She wouldn't be until she was able to have a few minutes to herself to deal with the reality that she was facing. She knew it would be better once Slade was gone. He didn't want a child and she was thirty-nine and pregnant. She had no idea what she was going to do.

She walked into her bedroom and found Slade standing in the doorway to her bathroom.

Crud.

She'd completely spaced on the fact that the pregnancy tests were still lined up on the counter.

"So, this is why you are dumping me?" he asked, gesturing to the tests.

"No, maybe. I just know that you're not interested in a family and unless all seven of those are defective, I'm definitely pregnant and it's your baby."

"This changes everything," he said.

"It most certainly doesn't," she said. "If you had felt differently, you would have already said so."

He shook his head. "No, I wouldn't have. We were talking possibilities. This is a reality. And there is no way I'm going to be that guy—the one who walks away from his kid. Oh, damn, this kid isn't going to have it easy."

She didn't know what Slade was referring to exactly, because he'd only once mentioned how hard his childhood was and somehow that was why he didn't want children. "Our child will be fine. We need to make choices that are best for the child, not what we want."

Because what she wanted was for Slade to suddenly confess he loved her and then demand a large fairy-tale wedding before she got too big for her dream dress. But that *was* a fairy tale and she knew it. Even if he did those things, she wouldn't be able to believe him. He'd been trying to talk her into continuing their affair, not starting a family.

"You're right. But everything we've seen with our work on the Coalition for Families shows that kids have a better quality of life when both parents are actively involved. We need to be making decisions together."

He had a point, but she wasn't ready to deal with this with him. Or anyone else. Her sister was still saying that Slade wasn't the right man for her. She'd had several concerned texts and emails from women and men on the various committees she served on, all warning her that Slade was bad news. And he was standing here looking panicked, yet trying to convince her that the child she carried should have both parents.

She just wasn't ready to deal with this. Not today.

Her phone started buzzing again, and she glanced down at it, shaking her head. Another media request for an interview. Slade came over and looked down at the phone.

"How many of these have you had today?"

"A million. That's an exaggeration, but it feels like that. I don't know what I'm going to do," she said. "I can't keep dodging them forever, and wearing a disguise every time I leave the house isn't going to work either. Eventually they're going to notice I'm pregnant and I don't know what to do."

Slade put his arm around her, and she let herself be pulled into his embrace, resting her head against his shoulder as he rubbed his hand down her back. His spicy aftershave made her pulse beat a little heavier, as did being held in his arms.

She wished she didn't react so quickly to him

each time he touched her. It made it hard for her to keep her perspective and be sensible.

He tipped her head with his finger under her chin and then rubbed his thumb over her jawline, which sent a tingle of awareness through her body. She parted her lips and then licked them as they were suddenly dry.

He groaned, then leaned down to kiss her, his mouth moving over hers slowly and deliberately. She turned more fully into his embrace, going up on tiptoe and twining her arms behind his neck and holding on to him. He tasted so good and she closed her eyes, letting the worries of the day disappear and allowing herself to just be in the moment.

When she was in Slade's arms, nothing else seemed to matter, and though she knew she couldn't stay there, she wanted to. But that wasn't realistic.

She broke the kiss and stepped away from him. She didn't know what to say, but she felt lost and she hated that. She'd always had a plan for her life. Even when it didn't work out the way she wanted, she was able to take steps to course-correct and get back to where she wanted to be.

But this thing with Slade was different. The man he was in real life blurred with the fantasy man that a part of her had been waiting for all her life and that made it harder to be sensible. *Ugh.*

"I have a solution," he said. "And I think it's one you'll like, because it's respectable and it will give the

media something to cover instead of your family's...
troubles."

"What do you have in mind?" she asked. She
wasn't going to pretend she didn't want to find a solution that would give her the best of both worlds, but
she knew how the media could be and she wanted to
maintain an image that was above reproach.

Something that Slade never had been, whether
fair or not. He'd always had to work double-time to
prove he wasn't in the mob.

"Let's get engaged."

Her heart fell to her stomach and she blinked,
trying very hard to maintain a poker face. His suggestion was the one thing she'd secretly been dreaming of. How could he have known?

But she knew there had to be a catch because
Slade wasn't the marrying kind. She looked at
him, sure he'd lost his mind or that she'd heard him
wrong. But he was smiling at her like he'd hung
the moon.

Even as the words left his mouth, he was questioning himself. But his emotions were roiling inside of him like a hurricane brewing in the Gulf of
Mexico and he felt like he was in a little dinghy,
trying to ride out the storm. Pregnant? Holy hell,
what were they going to do? He had never thought
about being a father.

He tried to focus his thoughts. One thing at a time.

Melinda was a respectable woman. She wouldn't embrace being single and pregnant until she had time to figure it out. Then it hit him. She tried to dump him after she found out she was having a baby. Did she think he'd be a horrible father? Was that why she was trying to walk away? She wasn't wrong, but damn that was a hit to his ego.

But temporarily engaged? Had he lost his ever-loving mind? Of course, Nonna would be thrilled. She adored Melinda. But if she found out Melinda was pregnant and he hadn't asked her to marry him, there would be hell to pay.

He wasn't the marrying kind. He had a lot of dark baggage inside of him. Still, what else could he do?

Panic washed over him like waves and he didn't like it. He hadn't allowed himself to be in a situation he couldn't control since he'd been fourteen. He was always in command of himself and the events around him.

Though nothing about this situation was normal.

He put his hands in the pockets of his trousers and stood there, trying to project a calm, in-control facade. But he was wigging out.

A *baby*?

A BABY!

He'd never wanted children, had always been careful until Melinda and now he was faced with a situation that he had to get out ahead of. He did it all the time at Conti Enterprises, he reminded himself.

And he would use those same winning techniques here. The one area of his life that he had always had complete control over was his role as CEO at Conti. It was the one time when he walked into a room and people talked about his reputation as an executive and not a rumored mobster's son.

He could do this.

Melinda needed him to be that man. To show her that he wasn't going to cut and run. They'd do this together, he told himself, even though he felt a tingle of fear run down his spine. What did he know about staying in a relationship?

And raising a child?

What did he know about being a father?

His pulse raced faster and harder than it had the one time he'd been sitting in the back of his dad's car when his father had gone to "take care of some business." That night had changed Slade forever and he had never been able to look at his father the same way again. It had cemented in Slade's mind that the life his father lived wasn't for him.

This was another big change. The kind that he had to take seriously. His child… A Bartelli. He needed to ensure that the child was safe from rivals and from his father's gang.

An engagement—a temporary engagement— seemed to be the best solution.

He told her so.

He saw the expression that flashed on her face

before she spoke. A combination of confusion and disappointment. "A temporary engagement? How is that a solution?"

"I know it sounds crazy but hear me out," he said. He'd always been famed for being quick on his feet, which was why he'd had so much success courting the media and driving the Conti business. Now he wasn't sure that winging it was the right thing to do. But there was no time for careful planning.

She shook her head. "I'm listening, Slade, but honestly, this is the craziest thing you've ever said to me."

"I agree," he admitted. "But this baby changes everything. You have enough to deal with already without having the media hounding you. I'm not throwing shade, but your family has been a hot mess lately. If we were engaged, our relationship will seem legit and it's a positive thing. It won't stop the speculation when you start showing a baby bump, but it will make it easier for me to be the point of contact. Trust me, I can frame it so they think we're head over heels for each other."

He knew he should throw out the word *love*, but he couldn't say that, not even to convince her. He didn't know if he loved her or if he would ever love her. Right now, he was focused on step one. Convince her to be his temporary fiancée and then they could move on to… Oh, my, the pregnancy.

For the first time, he looked at her belly and she

seemed the exact same to him. He would never have guessed she was pregnant from looking at her, but he'd seen the tests; he knew she was. He also knew she had to be losing her shit over it. Neither of them had expected this.

He'd used condoms every time except that one night…when once hadn't been enough and he'd been too into her to even think of reaching for one.

He expected her to come with more excuses, more reasons this was not a viable plan. Instead, she surprised him.

"How would it work?" she asked, moving over to the padded bench at the end of her bed and sitting down delicately on it. She crossed her legs as she looked over at him and he had to take a moment to gather his thoughts because she looked so pretty and unconsciously sexy. He knew she was in her serious mode so he couldn't make a pass at her, but he wanted to.

"I'm thinking we both go to dinner at my grandmother's tonight. Nonna already told me to bring you, so she's expecting us. I ask you to marry me, you say yes and we make an announcement to the media tomorrow."

"Why are we doing it now?" she asked.

He smiled. She was working through questions that some of the more persistent reporters might level at them. He liked this about her. She was a rule follower by nature, but she wasn't used to dealing with a world that liked to dwell in the gray area. But the problems with her father were making her more aware of it. So she knew the speed bumps they'd encounter.

"The photo in the *Chronicle* forced our hand," he said without needing much time to think. "We wanted to keep our relationship secret for a bit longer, but now that the cat's out of the bag, so to speak, we decided to go public."

She stood up and walked over to the window that afforded her a view of downtown and stood there with the September sunlight cascading over her, making her blond hair seem even brighter and giving her an ethereal glow. She looked down at the city and he wished he knew what she was thinking.

If she said no to this, he was sort of out of options. He couldn't stand to walk away from her and he certainly couldn't leave her on her own. He didn't know what his father might do if he found out about the grandchild. Slade kept calm because he knew that he would do whatever he had to in order to protect Melinda and their baby and keep them safe from everything and everyone.

Especially his father.

"So, what do you say?" he asked.

Melinda needed a minute… Okay, she needed more like several days to process this. Temporarily engaged? That didn't sound like something she wanted…or was it? At least she'd have time to think and Slade would provide a barrier between herself and the media. He'd also provide an excuse to avoid her family…just until she got her bearings again.

But that didn't really seem fair. Of all the things that she'd thought she'd encounter this morning when she woke up, this wasn't it.

"Okay. If we do this, how would it work? I mean, would we be pretending for a few months? And then I'd say I was pregnant, and you don't want a family and we'd break it off?" she asked. She needed to know all the rules for this engagement. She had to have parameters because obviously when she just went with her instincts, things happened. Unexpected things like a baby.

She still wasn't completely comprehending the pregnancy. She just wasn't the kind of girl—woman, she supposed she should say—who things like this happened to. She was the sensible twin. The quiet twin. The prim and proper twin. The actually-contemplating-a-temporary-engagement twin.

Oh, my stars. How am I going to handle this?

"Why don't we play it by ear?"

She shook her head. "No can do, buster. I need to know what's what, so I don't start to fall for the lie. It's easy for you because you never wanted a wife or a child, but I kind of always wanted a kid and a husband. I just don't want to let myself fall for something that's not real. So, if we are going to do this, I want to know when it ends and how."

He didn't like that. She could tell by the brief tightening of his mouth and narrowing of his eyes, but he covered it quickly with a flashing smile. "Of course, my darling, whatever you want. We'll sort out how it'll work. We just need some time."

"Your *darling*?"

"Unless you hate it," he said. "I think some endearments might help sell the whole head-over-heels thing."

"I don't think we have to do that," she said quickly. The last thing she wanted was Slade pitying her and pretending to love her. And he hadn't mentioned anything permanent before this or called her by a pet name. "We're both of an age where people will think we did this deliberately, not that it was an accident. I think it's better to play it like two rational, mature people."

He moved closer and she backed up till she felt the bed against the back of her knees. "Are you afraid of what will happen if we act like a couple in love?"

He stared at her with that intense gaze of his and she felt like he could see straight to her heart where her deepest fantasies resided. The fantasy of him turning into her white knight. That totally-improbable-but-also-sort-of-what-she'd-like fantasy. She wanted to look away, but she forced her gaze to hold his. "I've never been afraid of a man, Slade. I'm not going to start with you."

"Touché, darling. You are one tough cookie. That's why I have to constantly stay on my guard around you," he said.

"Stop flattering me. One of the things I liked about you was that you didn't treat me like everyone else does," she said, then realized she was saying too much. She didn't need to let him know that his seeing the real woman behind the preppy exterior had been part of why she'd let down her guard.

"Okay. How about this?" he said. "I'll go and leave you to your thoughts. I'll pick you up at seven for dinner with Nonna—unless you don't want to come?"

"I'll come. I'll see you at seven," she said.

"Text me if you make your decision. I want to talk to Nonna before anyone else knows," he said.

One of the many things that she liked about Slade was his closeness to his grandmother. It always made her wonder why he was so dead set against a relationship, given how tight the two of them were. "I will. I just need a little time to myself to sort this out. You arrived just after I'd taken the last test."

"I understand," he said, squeezing her shoulder. "Why did you get so many?"

She rolled her eyes to the side. "I wanted to be sure. You know they aren't totally accurate."

"I do know that," he said.

"Oh? Have you had a pregnancy scare before?" she asked.

"Not since I was twenty. After that one, I decided that I needed to be more careful," he admitted.

"I've never had one before this," she said.

He laughed but it was dry. "I guess that's one more thing that makes me different from the rest."

She knew he was referencing his rumored mob boss family ties and she couldn't help but get upset for him. She might not want to be temporarily engaged, but that had nothing to do with how others thought of him.

"What makes you different, Slade Bartelli, is that you are genuine and never put on airs the way so many other men I've met do. You're honest and true and you don't let anything stand in your way. I've never met a man like you."

He looked away from her and when he turned back, he nodded. "I don't know that I'm as good as you just made me sound, but you do make me want to be a better man."

"I can't imagine how you'd be better than you are now," she said. He was a good man because he was constantly weighing the consequences for every decision. She liked that about him, but that didn't mean she wanted to find herself trapped in a temporary engagement to him. She knew, though, that if he'd asked her, he'd already run some sort of calculation in his head and this was the best solution.

She wanted to believe that it was because he wanted to protect her, but a big part of her was afraid it had more to do with him. Slade had worked so hard to prove he was better than his gangster daddy; the last thing he'd want was a baby mama who was pushing forty.

Slade knew the battle he always waged within himself. He knew he was always one footfall away from stepping over the line and becoming Carlo's son. But he fought it. The thing was, when he was with Melinda it was easier. She made the battle raging inside of him not as intense, and he didn't want to let that go.

Of course, now that she was pregnant that changed things a bit. He was panicking and doing his usual bid to ignore it and it was almost working.

Or had been until she'd decided that defending him to himself was the thing to do. She had an innate goodness that he'd rarely encountered in anyone before, even his nonna. Philomena Conti was a very kind and nurturing woman, but she was also tough as nails, having to make some hard decisions running the Conti empire since her husband's premature death in Vietnam in the 70s. Slade had taken the helm on his twenty-eighth birthday.

Melinda seemed the type of woman who'd never had to make those choices or if she had made them, the impact hadn't tainted her.

She wasn't naive or anything like that. She could hold her own with anyone, but she did it in a way that made the person she was going toe-to-toe with wish they'd never upset her.

He needed to stop extolling her virtues. He needed to get out of her condo. Turning to the bedroom door, he threw over his shoulder, "I'll see you at seven."

"I might jot down a few ideas for how this temporary engagement will work and then text it over to you," she said, following him. "Will that be okay?"

No. He didn't want a bunch of rules he had to follow. He really didn't do well with that type of thing. But she'd said she needed it and he was trying to protect her, keep his grandmother happy and his father far away from her, so he was going to have to go along with her ideas. "Sure, that would be fine. Send it when you have it ready."

He walked out of her bedroom but when he got to the front door, she reached out and caught his hand, squeezing it. "We're going to figure this out and give this kid the best shot it has for a great life. I really believe in us."

"Great." He realized he sounded a bit sarcastic, which suited his mood that was quickly heading south. "Once we know what we're doing, I'm sure it will make us both feel more confident."

But he wasn't sure. He had come from a mob family, she had come from a broken family and her mom was rumored to have had an affair with another man. Both of them were almost forty and had spent the bulk of their lives alone. That had to mean something.

Or else it was just him going insane.

"Thanks for being so chill about this," she said. "And for giving me the space I need."

"Of course," he said, pulling her close and kissing her. But it was different now. His mind reeled with all the things that were implied in this embrace. She was carrying his baby, she wasn't his and for the first time that mattered to him.

He'd never been one of those guys who had to have a woman committed to him, but thinking about Melinda walking away—which she might do—he felt a need to put on the charm and convince her to stay.

Maybe he should take her to bed. She never said no to him when they were intimate. He tried to deepen the kiss, angling his head to the side and sliding his hands down her back to cup her butt and pull her more fully against him, but she twisted her head away.

She turned back to face him, and their eyes met. "That's a surefire way to muddle my thinking."

"And a surefire way to cement mine," he said.

"This can't just be sex anymore. It's not just the two of us anymore," she said.

That's why he wanted sex. He needed it, so

he could lie to himself and convince himself that nothing had changed between them. That once he walked out the door, things were going to stay okay. But he knew they wouldn't. Nothing was going to be like it was before.

It wasn't the first time his life had done one of these huge shifts and to be honest, he'd hated it last time, so he was pretty damned sure he wasn't going to love it now.

But this was Melinda and she deserved the best he had to give. Kissing her on her forehead, he let her go and stepped away. "You're right. I'll see you later."

He walked out her front door and down the hall toward the elevator, making sure he didn't hesitate until he was out of her sight. Then he paused. For the first time since he'd seen all those pregnancy tests on the bathroom counter, he allowed his emotions free rein. His hands shook and he had that nervous sensation in the pit of his stomach. A heady cocktail of both fear and excitement.

A baby.

His baby.

His and Melinda's.

He should take a page out of her planner and go make some notes on what to do, but he didn't need that. His list was pretty damn short. Make sure the kid was nothing like his dad.

Five

As soon as Slade was gone, Melinda called her sister. Her phone went to voice mail, which it did a lot lately. She was worried about Angela. It was hard being in love with a man their father hated. Ryder Currin. The man who many believed had had an affair with their mother and who had framed their father for embezzling. But Angela loved him, and as a woman who was pregnant with her lover's baby, Melinda got it. The heart didn't always follow the most well-laid plans.

She almost let herself be distracted by that. Almost let herself focus on her twin instead of the very big problem in front of her. It would be so much easier to try to deal with Angela's issues instead of her own.

Her phone pinged with a reminder and she glanced down to see she had forty minutes to get to the board meeting for Help Houston Read. It was a charity that she had cofounded with one of her sorority sisters almost ten years ago. They worked on making sure that every kid had a library of books at home. It was an idea they'd borrowed from Dolly Parton, who had started doing it in her home state of Tennessee.

She hurried into her bedroom, showered and changed back into her A-line skirt and blouse with the bow at the collar. She took her hair down from its ponytail and then fluffed it around her face before grabbing her catchall bag, a Louis Vuitton that had been her gift to herself when she'd started the foundation. She made sure she had her planner and notepad, ignored the pregnancy tests on the bathroom counter and walked out the door.

She took the elevator to the ground floor and walked quickly through the lobby. There were no photographers waiting and the doorman smiled at her as she approached.

"Mr. Bartelli took care of the scavengers, so it's all clear," Johnny said.

"Thank you for letting me know," she said, putting on her wide-frame cat's-eye sunglasses as she stepped out into the Houston sun. She kept her head held high and her posture straight as she walked to her car. It was a VW Passat because she liked small cars that weren't too ostentatious.

She made good time to her meeting and realized once she was seated in the conference room with a large glass of sweet tea in her tumbler that she'd almost forgotten about Slade, the engagement and the baby. Almost.

"Hiya, Melinda," Carly said, walking into the room with a smile on her face. Her sorority sister and co-founder was always someone she was happy to see. "I guess I don't need to ask if you had a good time at the opera last night."

"Girl, you don't even know the half of it," Melinda said. "I have no idea how that picture got into the *Chronicle*."

"He's big news for that page and you are seldom seen outside of charity events, so they probably felt like they got the scoop of a lifetime," Carly said.

"They did."

"How are you holding up? I know that kind of publicity isn't your thing."

"It's not, but I'm doing okay," she said. Then she remembered that Slade wanted them to be engaged. She hadn't decided yet, but she knew she should start laying the groundwork in case they did it. "We've been dating for a while."

"I suspected you had a new man but had no idea it was Slade Bartelli. That is one hot-looking man."

She blushed. He was a hot-looking man and she

made no bones that she liked the way his ass looked in his custom-made tuxedo, but she also liked the way he made her feel like what she was saying was important. Whenever they were out together, she had never seen Slade looking at another woman or being distracted by his phone—which was saying something because his phone pinged constantly with updates, messages and media alerts. But when he was on a date with her, he made her his priority.

"He is," she said. "No denying it."

"But you're not usually the type to fall for a great pair of biceps. Remember Antonio? He tried for months to get you to go out with him," Carly said, sitting down across from her and taking her laptop from her bag.

Melinda already had her laptop set up and glanced down at the screen as a notification popped up in the right corner, letting her know that she had over a hundred new social media tags.

Ugh.

"Antonio was all smoke and mirrors. Sure, he looked hot but the man had never heard of Dalí. Let's face it, if you're on the art council, you should at least have heard the name before," Melinda said.

"Agreed. Not saying you should have hooked up with Antonio. I'm simply curious why Slade," Carly said.

"He's smart and funny and sexy. I mean, there is a part of me that knows there is a dark side to him, but when I'm with him, he seems…well, too good to be true," she admitted. She knew that no man was perfect and yet when she was with Slade, everything seemed ideal.

"How long have y'all been dating? You know how it is when a relationship is new," Carly said.

"Not too long. A little over six weeks," Melinda said. Her friend had a point. The relationship was new. She'd been trying to be her best self as Slade was probably doing as well.

"Wait until you hit your first road bump and see how he reacts," Carly said. "That will give you the measure of the man."

Carly had a point, which she allowed herself to think about as the rest of the committee slowly came into the conference room. The pregnancy should have ruffled Slade. Shown her more of the real man behind the gentlemanly image he'd been portraying for her.

But it hadn't.

Other than his temporary engagement idea, but even that had been framed in a way to benefit her.

It made her wonder if he was hiding something.

Something dark and dangerous.

Something…Bartelli family–related.

Though Slade had always assured her he had no part in his father's business, there was an edge to the man who was her baby's father that she'd never allowed herself to dwell on. Perhaps it was time she did.

* * *

Slade was ready for the press conference to discuss his latest project. Conti Enterprises was a multinational business, the bulk of which was made up of shopping malls and a global shipping company. Their malls were the best and the most popular destinations around the world.

His assistant had texted him the talking points in the note function of his phone and Slade was ready to do this. He smiled and then jumped up and down a few times. Jumping helped quell his nervous energy. He had learned early on that when he was nervous, he looked like he was hiding something and the media always assumed it was something illegal.

He shook his head, put his shoulders back and reminded himself he was the biggest badass in Houston before going into the press conference. In the audience, he saw many familiar faces but also a few reporters he'd never seen before and one or two photographers he was sure were paparazzi.

He gave his prepared remarks, talking about an innovative new shipping design platform they'd be using going forward that would reduce their carbon footprint and create more jobs in areas that needed them. The project had been close to his heart for a while, so he was glad to see it finally fully operational.

"I'll be happy to take any questions now," he said.

"Are you and Melinda Perry a couple now?"

"I'd rather talk about the new shipping platform," he said.

"I have your press release and my society editor asked me to find out what's the deal with Melinda Perry. She's usually not in the news, and we know that her family has been at the center of some…let's say, interesting issues lately."

"Melinda and I serve together on a committee for the arts and we have been dating, but you know I don't really like to talk too much about my personal life."

"So I can confirm you are a couple?"

"Sure," he said, starting to feel a little hot under the collar as he wasn't 100 percent sure what Melinda wanted him to say. But he decided to just give them enough to hopefully make the story die down.

"Do you think you are more acceptable to her now that her father is out of jail but still under suspicion for murder?" another reporter asked.

"I'm willing to answer questions that are legit, but I won't trade in gossip. I've never been one to credit alleged accusations or anonymous tips. Melinda Perry is the most upright and honest woman I know," he said. "Melinda and I aren't our parents and neither of us should be in any way associated with any allegations against our fathers."

"Well, that's a nice thought but let's face it, she has a lot of money at her disposal to do all of her charitable work and it had to come from somewhere. There's bound to be questions about—"

"Enough. If you ever met Melinda, you would know that she's not the type of person who would engage in any criminal activity. For years, I've lived under the cloud of being a Bartelli, so I know what it's like to be unfairly tainted by association. Melinda doesn't deserve this. And I'm done taking questions for today."

He turned and left the room, knowing he could have handled that last part better but really he'd almost lost his temper. He didn't mind getting the side-eye himself; he'd grown up being treated that way. He'd been the kid that most parents didn't want as a friend for their own child. He'd been denied several things before he made his own name for himself.

It hadn't been easy.

But Melinda shouldn't have to be the one to deal with that. He was tempted to go and see Sterling Perry and tell the man to step up and be the father that Melinda needed him to be, but Slade knew that men like Sterling put themselves first. There was a cloud of suspicion around him and he should be taking steps to make sure his children weren't painted with the same brush, but instead he was busy trying to blame his rival Ryder Currin in the media.

His assistant was waiting for him in the hallway. "I'm sorry about that. I gave them the talking points and did reiterate that you'd only be taking questions about the new shipping information."

He nodded. "It's not your fault. You know how they can be. I need you to reach out to Melinda's assistant and get her schedule. I think there is a good chance that she's going to have more paparazzi on her tail than she expected," he said.

His assistant nodded and left, and Slade went into his office and fought the urge to put his fist through the wall. The timing of that kiss last night showing up in the paper couldn't have been worse for the two of them. Her family name was tarnished, and she had enough to deal with without having to answer questions about the two of them.

And the baby.

He couldn't forget the child that she was carrying. The one that he wasn't sure he wanted to raise but knew he had to protect. And it seemed as if it wasn't just the Bartelli side that threatened Melinda and their baby, but also the Perrys. He needed information and one of his old friends Will Brady had just settled down in Royal, so he might have some intel that could help Slade understand what was going on.

Will was a computer genius and occasionally Slade hired him to dig around on the internet and find information before he did business with someone he didn't know.

He texted Will and asked him to look into the Sterling Perry thing. Then resisted the urge to text

Melinda. She said she'd get back to him if and when she'd made her decision and she'd always been a woman of her word.

But that didn't ease the feeling in his gut that something bad was about to happen. He thought about the message his assistant had given him from his dad earlier. Was his father the cause of the bad feeling? Or was it simply that for the first time in his life, he had to look out for someone else and he wasn't sure he could protect Melinda?

Melinda hit the mute button on her phone when her dad's number popped up. He was the last person she wanted to talk to. She'd been doing her best to be there for him and to help him through this trying time, but he hadn't approved of her and Slade being on the same committee and she was pretty sure he was about to issue some sort of autocratic decree regarding her and Slade. And as much as she always tried to frame her father's overbearing ways as the only way he knew how to love her, she wasn't in the mood to be placating.

The meeting had gone well but there had been paparazzi and gossip bloggers waiting when she'd exited, and it had taken all of her willpower to just smile and walk calmly around them and not run for her car like she wanted to.

She knew that Slade thought an engagement would be a nice barrier between her and the media, and she had to be honest and admit she was beginning to believe that it would work. With her dad just out of jail on the dropped embezzlement charges, and the rumors swirling that he might know more about the Vincent Hamm murder, and her own scandalous embrace captured at the opera, maybe an engagement would be just the thing to make them all lose interest.

"Ms. Perry, can you confirm that you are dating Slade Bartelli?"

She kept walking, tried to keep her shoulders straight and her head up. Her personal life was no one's business but her own. She hadn't used the media to build her business or her charities. She'd done it through hard work.

"Don't want to talk about that?" the guy said. "What about the rumor that your father is a suspect in the Vincent Hamm murder? Want to discuss that?"

She took a deep breath. She knew that engaging the guy would be akin to trying to be reasonable with a quack on social media. Whatever she said or didn't say he was going to spin to fit his own narrative.

"You always were the boring Perry. Interesting that you are now the one in the spotlight. Some think it's because you're trying to cover for your father and the illegal activities of Slade Bartelli."

That hit a nerve. She lost her temper, turning

on her heel to confront the portly man following so closely behind her. "I can see, sir, that you are a man with very little manners and probably even less brain, so I'm going to speak slowly and use small words, so you don't get confused. My father is a good man who hasn't done anything wrong. And Slade has spent his entire life being more transparent about every dealing he's ever had than most businesses you consider legitimate. You can make stuff up about them all day, but in the end, it will only prove that you're a complete moron. That's all I have to say."

She turned back around, hurried to her car, got inside and turned the air conditioner on full blast so that maybe it would cool her down. She put her sunglasses on and slowly drove out of the parking lot despite the fact that she wanted to speed away. She wanted to race out of Houston and keep driving north until she reached Oklahoma. Someplace where no one would know her and she could find some peace and quiet.

It was impossible to say that she needed time to think away from Slade when everyone she encountered kept bringing him up. She pulled into the CVS parking lot at the next block and drove around back and just parked the car. She put her head on the steering wheel and closed her eyes.

In all her days, she'd never expected her family name to be raked through the mud. She had also never thought that she'd be pregnant and having an affair with a bad boy…man. But Slade wasn't a bad man.

She wished there were some way she could be Slade's temporary fiancée and not fall in love with him. But she knew herself. She couldn't walk around telling people they were getting married and not fantasize about it.

In her mind, she easily pictured the wedding dress she'd choose—a simple Givenchy satin gown with a ballet neckline and fitted bodice with a flowing skirt. She could picture it in her mind and that was a mistake. *Temporary*, she reminded herself. That was all he'd offered her.

Something to get her through the odious reporters who wouldn't stop with their questions.

And unless she really did leave Texas, there was no way she was going to be able to distance herself from Slade. Normally she'd ask Angela for advice, but her sister wasn't returning her calls at the moment and her father… Well, he'd never been an advice giver.

This decision was going to be all on her.

And to be honest, she knew what she was going to do. Had known since the moment that he'd said those ridiculous sweet words. She was going to say yes and become Slade Bartelli's fiancée in the eyes of Houston and the world. Everyone would see a couple who cared deeply for each other and had decided to commit their lives to one another. She felt tears burn her eyes because it was the secret dream she'd always harbored. But maybe it was time to be realistic. Maybe this temporary thing with Slade was all she'd have when it came to men. But she would have a child.

A family of her own.

One where no one was demanding. She and the child would have each other. Already Melinda felt better. And Angela. The child would have a wonderful auntie too. And if sometimes Melinda wished that things had worked out differently, then she would keep that to herself. She lifted her head off the steering wheel, wiped her eyes and picked up her phone.

This was a business deal. A PR stunt to distract the society reporters and bloggers, and when the heat died down, they would go back to their normal lives. Slade had been honest about not wanting a family and she knew that at the end of the day, she'd be raising the child on her own.

She was okay with that.

Really, she was.

And maybe if she repeated it often enough to herself, she'd start to believe it.

<u>Six</u>

Dinner at Philomena Conti's house was something that Melinda always looked forward to. Given all the craziness in her life currently, she definitely needed it tonight. She and Slade had postponed the previous week. She just hadn't been ready to talk to anyone about the engagement until they'd had time to sort a few details out. It had been a week since the news of her and Slade had broken, and she was no closer to figuring out what to do next now than she had been then.

"Jeeves, play my soothing playlist."

"Playing your soothing playlist," the in-home automated assistant said.

Melinda went back to getting ready, thinking

about Philomena. She had a joie de vivre that drew people to her. Over the years since they had started serving on the art council together, Melinda had found her to be almost a kindred spirit.

Philomena lived her life in a bolder way than Melinda did, but at their core, they both sought to help others and surrounded themselves with nice people. She'd debated a number of times about driving herself versus letting Slade pick her up and, in the end, since she'd decided to go ahead with the engagement, he would be driving her.

As she zipped herself into a simple navy sheath dress with ruffles at the shoulders, she realized that she wouldn't have that much longer before she might not be able to wear it. She had gone to Katy, a suburb of Houston, and its fabulous bookstore to pick up a few books on pregnancy and then, because she couldn't resist, had tossed a few romance novels into her basket as well. She wasn't one of those people who went into a bookstore and came out with one book. It was always an armful.

Glancing at her Cartier gold-and-steel watch, she knew she needed to keep moving and not stop and check out the books on her nightstand. She was already going to be at least ten minutes late, something her own grandmother had said was key to making a man understand how much time she'd put into getting ready for him. To be honest, she was usually ready on time and had to stall for ten minutes.

But today was different. And how! She went back to the vanity to put her long blond hair into a chignon and then touched up her makeup. She realized she was a little bit stressed and trying to look perfect.

But why?

This wasn't real. She had to remember that. Slade wanted them to get through these troubled waters before they talked about the future. But the baby and the media left them with no choice other than to be engaged. Right? But it was hard. Harder than she'd imagined.

"I can do this, can't I, Pixie?" she asked the dog, who came over and danced around her feet.

Melinda reached down and scooped her up. Pixie put her front paws on Melinda's chest, her tail wagging as Melinda petted her. She wished that the world were as easy to please as this little dog.

She kissed Pixie on the nose and then set her back on the floor. That was a nice break from her worrying, but now she was back to it.

She wanted any photos taken of the two of them to look real. The kind of image that would hang on the wall in a house in tony River Oaks. But that wasn't the endgame here. They were both trying to salvage a situation that was going from bad to worse with her reputation and Slade's always scandalous one.

She tried to just leave her appearance as it was,

but she couldn't do it. Philomena would definitely know something was up if Melinda wasn't wearing her pearls and princess-cut diamond stud earrings. They were her formal wear go-tos, which her friend would know.

She was struggling with lying to Philomena and her sister. She didn't mind letting the society bloggers and reporters believe something that wasn't true, or even her father. But her twin? That was much harder. And while she and Angela didn't share every detail of their lives, this was a big rock. One of the things that if it were real, she'd be giddily over-sharing every detail with her sister.

Instead… Well, to be fair, Angela had been incommunicado all day, so that did make it easier to keep from having to tell her she was going to get engaged. That was sort of okay too, because Angela had had a lot of gossip swirling around her and Melinda was trying to distance herself from that.

She supposed tonight at Philomena's house would be the test if she could pull off the temporary engagement with sincerity. She'd never been a good poker player or actress. She could be cordial to strangers but her friends always knew where they stood with her. If they could convince Slade's grandmother they were the real deal, the rest of the world would be easy.

Sure, it would be. But one thing at a time. That

was how she'd been successful at accomplishing as much as she had in her life.

When the doorbell rang, Pixie jumped up from her bed and started barking as she raced to the door. Melinda glanced at her watch; Slade was twenty minutes early. She was ready, and keeping him waiting today wasn't going to happen. She wanted to discuss the engagement and make it clear he couldn't live with her, as he'd suggested. She'd written down the things she needed to ensure didn't happen, so she wouldn't fall for the fairy tale.

Number one: no more sex.

Number two: no living together.

Number three: don't fall in love.

She took a deep breath. She wasn't going to mention number three to him. That one was for her eyes only. A reminder to not let herself believe the temporary fix.

No sex was going to be a hard sell for both of them. He turned her on, and she had gotten used to sleeping with him. But she wanted to come out of this thing between her and Slade with as much of her soul intact as she could. And she knew herself well enough to know that if she slept with him or lived with him, then it was going to be hard not to fall in love with him.

She walked through her condo slowly and glanced at the video monitor before opening the door. Slade looked so good in a dinner jacket and tie that her heart started racing. His dark hair was slicked back the way he styled it for formal events and he'd shaved—Philomena didn't care for stubble.

She took a deep breath to center herself before she opened the door. Pixie greeted him with some doggy kisses on his leg and Slade bent over to pet her before he came into the condo.

She took a few steps back, realizing how much taller he was than her. Normally she always had on heels and it wasn't often she stood this close to him in bare feet.

"I know I'm early but I figured we should have a game plan before we head to dinner," he said.

She just nodded as she realized that not falling for him was going to be a lot harder than she'd previously thought. Mainly because she already was halfway in love with him.

Slade had never struggled so much with any decision and he guessed that was one thing he could thank his father for. He'd always been very focused on not following in the old man's footsteps that most of his choices were easy. But this one… Well, it was like the past coming back to haunt him.

His parents had had a marriage of necessity. His mom had become pregnant with him and, bowing to the pressure of the Conti family, Carlo Bartelli had married his mother. But the marriage hadn't worked out and had led to some very unhappy decisions by both of his parents.

Right now, the back of his neck felt tight, and as much as he wanted to be the cool and suave man he liked to think he usually was, he'd never felt more out of his depth. The engagement was simply for her protection, he reminded himself. He'd promised himself to never marry and that promise wasn't one he was willing to break.

Even for Melinda.

She looked breathtakingly lovely as she stood there in her blue dress and bare feet. It was all he could do not to sweep her up in his arms and carry her to bed. But he knew that was a temporary distraction and not what was needed right now. He rubbed the back of his neck to get rid of the tension there, but it didn't help.

"Would you like something to drink?"

"Hard liquor might be nice, but I don't think Nonna would appreciate it," he said. "So I'm fine."

"She definitely wouldn't. Okay, so let's sit down and talk this out," she said, leading the way into her formal living room and taking a seat on the armchair, leaving the love seat for him.

The room was so feminine with delicate-looking furniture and more flowers and stripes than he had ever seen before. It was classy and elegant and a part of him always felt out of place here, as he knew he was neither of those things.

"First, thank you."

"You're welcome," he said, "but for what?"

"Trying to help me by suggesting we get engaged and then giving me time to think it over," she said, twisting her fingers together.

"It was the least I could do."

"It wasn't and I appreciate it. I've thought about your suggestion that we live together, and I must say I don't think that will work for me. I'm too used to being alone and I need this time to get ready for the baby," she said.

"Fair enough," he said, feeling a bit hurt, but he reminded himself that he didn't want to raise a child. "That's probably for the best, as I'll be a financial support for you and the child but not physically in your life."

Her mouth tightened but she nodded after a moment. "Right. So we should set an end date for this engagement. I'm thinking three months? That's enough time for the interest in me to die down and hopefully Daddy's mess will be sorted by then."

Three months. That was longer than any of his previous relationships, and yet with Melinda, it almost felt too short. Which meant it was perfect. "Why don't we reassess the situation then? If we need to keep it going, then we will. And it will be before Christmas, so that will give the society bloggers something else to write about."

"Okay." She bit her lower lip and turned her head

away. "This next thing is… Well, it's awkward so I'm just going to say it. I think we should definitely try to keep it platonic from here on out."

Hell, no.

"I'm listening," he said instead.

"The thing is I don't know what my body is going to be doing… I haven't had a chance to read any of the books I picked up today," she said. "Plus, you and I should be focused on keeping up appearances when we're out at events but in our private lives, we should be trying to work out how our lives will be after the baby comes. I know you don't want to be a part of the child's life…so us hooking up is probably not a good idea."

He leaned back against the love seat and pretended to be considering her idea. And he was doing just that, but he was also trying to manage the realization that this pregnancy had changed everything. He couldn't end the relationship with Melinda the way he normally would have, letting it trickle off and then having one big explosive sexual encounter at the end before he walked away. Instead, he had to end it now and then pretend it wasn't over.

He was about to just walk away from everything when his phone vibrated in his pocket and he got a notification of a new post about himself and Melinda. He couldn't leave her to face this alone. It was the least he could do for her and for that child she was carrying.

He knew he had to do whatever he could to make them as safe as possible. If that meant agreeing to no sex, he'd do it. But he suspected she wouldn't find that any easier than he would. There was something between them that Slade hadn't experienced before. An attraction that made it impossible for them to stay apart.

"Okay," he finally said. "But if you change your mind, let me know."

She gave him one of those unexpected grins of hers that made his pulse race. "Honey, you'll be the first to know."

He laughed as she intended him to but inside, he was beginning to wonder if he'd made a huge mistake in ever asking her out. She'd been different and he'd thought that meant something exciting. But maybe it had been dangerous.

Nonna Conti was seventy-eight but looked more like she was fifty-eight. She had a trim figure that she kept by playing tennis three times a week, something Slade had confided she did as much for the gossip as the exercise. Her hair was a deep auburn color and always perfectly coiffed. She smiled warmly at Melinda as they entered her house and swept her up in a big hug.

The entry to the palatial neoclassical River Oaks mansion was all Ferrara marble. It was ivory and shot with gold and had a thick four-inch panel of dark brown marble that framed the entryway. Her designer had hung luxurious gold and white curtains in alternating panels along the wall that was framed with hand-carved molding. There was a thick carpet in the center that led to the sitting room.

The sitting room followed the same design but instead of the hanging panels, there were alternating mirrors, which made the room seem even larger and reminded Melinda of Versailles but not as gold.

After the day she'd had, she just let herself enjoy the hug and soak up the joy and affection from the older woman. Most days, Melinda didn't let herself dwell on the fact that she really missed her mom over the last ten years since she'd died, but today she had reached for the phone more than once to call her.

"It's so good to see you. You look cute as a button as always. I had Henri mix us up some gin and tonics and he's waiting in the sitting room with them," Philomena said, turning to greet her grandson.

Oh, it wasn't going to be as easy to hide the pregnancy as she'd wanted it to be. Obviously, she couldn't drink gin and tonic but Slade sort of indicated with his head for her to go ahead to the sitting room, which she did. She knew Henri, the butler, would be circumspect about her choice if she had a quiet word with him.

She heard Slade telling his grandmother about the opera as she rounded the corner and walked into the sitting room. They were the first of Philomena's guests to arrive, so the room was empty except for the butler, who wore a crisp white jacket and black trousers.

The bar was opulent like the rest of the room and Henri looked like he was a throwback to another age, standing there ready to serve the guests. At last year's Boots and Bangles charity gala, Philomena had asked Henri to volunteer to be one of the silent auction prizes and he'd agreed. She'd paid the fee for him to be someone's butler for the day, so he wasn't out his salary.

"Hello, Miss Melinda. We have your favorite tonight," he said, reaching for the pitcher as she walked over to him.

"Thanks so much, Henri, that means the world to me. But my stomach is acting up today—probably a few too many last night. Would you mind keeping mine just tonic but discreetly?" she asked.

"No problem, ma'am," he said with a wink as he reached to the second shelf of the bar cart and poured just tonic into her highball glass and added a twist of lime as a garnish.

"Thank you," she said, taking her drink from him and giving him a warm smile.

She moved away from the bar cart as Philomena and Slade entered the room. Henri poured them each a drink and then they joined her in one of the seating areas in the massive room. Slade took the spot next to her on one of the love seats and Philomena sat in what Melinda privately referred to as her throne chair. It was a high-backed padded chair upholstered in a deep purple brocade, which complemented the opulent marble, cream and gold room. It was higher than the other seats in the room and gave Philomena the air of holding court once she was perched there.

"Slade tells me the opera was excellent. I saw from the *Chronicle* that you two are getting on well," Philomena said.

Melinda felt herself blushing at that comment, but she wasn't embarrassed. They might be doing the temporary engagement thing but her feelings for Slade were real. "You knew we were seeing each other."

"I'd hoped you were. Now the world knows. Even though it did make things a bit awkward for the two of you," she admitted.

It had only been after Philomena had encouraged her to give her grandson a chance to prove he was more than the media made him out to be that Melinda had accepted her first date with him.

"Actually, Nonna, we are getting along so well that I asked Melinda to marry me and she said yes."

"You did what?"

"Nonna, I asked Melinda to marry me and she said yes."

"Philomena, is that okay?" Melinda asked. Given the mess that her family continued to be embroiled in lately, she wouldn't be surprised if the society matron wanted someone more respectable for her grandson.

"Oh, I adore you, Melinda, but my grandson had always said he was never getting married," Philomena said, looking over at Slade.

"Nonna, I might have felt that way before meeting Melinda. She's the kind of woman that makes a man realize what's important, so I asked her to marry me and she said yes. We'd like your blessing."

"You have it. Congratulations! Henri, champagne, please," Philomena said, but Henri had already started moving toward the butler's pantry and fully stocked bar. "Did he do something super romantic?"

Crappola. She hadn't thought about this and she should have. She was off her game and she blamed the pregnancy and the scandals that kept dogging her family. It seemed as if each time they got one thing sorted, something else popped up. She should have known people were going to ask about his proposal and they hadn't worked out anything. And let's face it, she couldn't say he saw all those pregnancy tests in the bathroom and said "Let's get temporarily engaged."

She glanced at Slade, who must have read the panic on her face because he reached over and took her hand in his. "Well, Nonna, if you must know,

I took her to the place where we had our first kiss and then went down on one knee."

She felt her heart catch in her throat. That would have been a very romantic gesture. The kind of thing that she'd always dreamed of. But men who were "doing the right thing" for their girlfriend's reputation didn't make gestures like that.

"Well-done, *Tesoro*. I knew you had it in you," she said. "You just were waiting for the right woman to come along."

"I definitely was," he said, keeping hold of her hand.

"And the ring?" Philomena asked.

Melinda would have pulled her hand back if Slade hadn't been holding it but he rubbed his thumb over her knuckles, which sent a sensual shiver up her arm.

He might be Philomena's *Tesoro*—treasure—but right now she wasn't so sure.

"I was hoping to speak to you privately about that matter tonight," he said.

"After we have a toast and some more guests arrive," Philomena said with a twinkle in her eyes. "You've made me very happy tonight, *Tesoro*. You know, I may have pushed him to take my seat on the art council because I wanted him to meet you. I'm glad to see he picked up my hints. I knew you two would be perfect for each other."

What?

Now the temporary engagement made more

sense, she thought, as she tugged her hand from his. Had he only asked her out to please his demanding grandmother? Was he protecting her from the bad press and helping to repair her reputation after the scandals that kept consuming the Perry family only to please his grandmother?

She was disappointed and mad at herself for letting him deceive her. But she knew the real blame lay with herself. She'd been the one making him into a better man than he was. He'd told her he didn't want a wife or child and she'd believed him, but secretly she hoped he'd change his mind. Now she had changed hers.

Seven

The dinner party was comprised of polite society members who, though they seemed curious about her and Slade, didn't ask them anything directly. The dining room was comprised of a long table that seated sixteen and a smaller round table that seated only eight. Philomena reserved the round table for herself and her specially invited guests. Slade and Philomena had disappeared for a few moments when the first guests arrived and when he came back, he tried to get a few minutes alone with Melinda, but she refused.

Instead, she pushed away all of the doubt and troubles of the day and socialized the way she'd been raised to. In fact, as the evening drew to a close with after-dinner drinks and a three-piece ensemble playing classical music, she thought she'd done a good job of camouflaging the fact that she was mad and hurt.

Finally, as the other guests started to leave, she faked a yawn and gave a tight smile to Slade. "It's getting kind of late. I think I'll get a taxi home."

"I'll take you," he said.

"You don't have to."

"Oh, I definitely do. I can tell you have something to say to me," he said, putting his hand on the small of her back to direct her toward his grandmother. While the gesture was one she normally liked, tonight she didn't. She was mad. Hurt that she'd never even had a thought that Philomena was setting them up. She was angry that she'd played an unwitting part in her scheme by getting pregnant.

She took quick steps to increase the distance between them, but he just kept up with her, curling his hand around her waist to stop her. She turned quickly to glare at him, but he just smiled at her and said quietly, "We have to keep up appearances."

She realized he was right. The last thing she wanted was to fuel more speculation about the two of them. It didn't matter if she was angry. Her number one goal now was to drop off the radar of the society bloggers. After that happened, she could deal with everything else.

"Sorry, darling," she said loud enough that others in the room could hear her. "I've got a wicked headache."

Then she leaned in, heard his quick intake of breath as she ran her fingers along the column of his neck in a caress she knew turned him on and then kissed him, quickly but deeply, before turning back toward Philomena.

She saw speculation in the other woman's eyes, but Melinda was done with the Conti-Bartelli clan tonight.

"Thank you for a wonderful dinner, Philomena. I loved it," she said, kissing the older woman on the cheek before she started to turn away.

"You're welcome, Melinda," Philomena said, catching her wrist before she could leave. "I'd love it if you could join me for lunch on Friday."

She started to say no, but Philomena lifted one eyebrow and Melinda realized this was a summons. "I'll have to check my schedule. If not Friday, perhaps Monday."

"That would be nice. I'll have Henri follow up with your assistant," she said. Then she pulled Melinda close and gave her a warm hug. "Congratulations again. I'm so glad you are going to be a part of the family."

She hugged Philomena back, a part of her dying inside that none of this was real. Had she made the decision to agree to this engagement too quickly? It was beginning to feel like she had.

"Me too," she said, turning away quickly so that Slade could say his goodbyes. She walked through the room saying goodbye to a few other friends.

Slade followed her through the house to the front door, his footsteps loud behind her as she walked. She took her purse from the antique sideboard where it was waiting for her. Henri was very good about anticipating any guests' needs.

As soon as they were outside, she glanced up at the September evening sky. God, the sky was big tonight. A half-moon shone down on them and stars and satellites twinkled in the night sky. She took a deep breath and felt some of her anger seep away.

"I'm sorry you had to hear about Nonna trying to set us up the way you did," he said once they were in the car and heading back toward downtown and her condo.

"It was a surprise," she admitted. "Are you planning to actually marry me?"

"No."

His answer was so quick and almost forceful. Well, there it was, she thought. Was he lying to everyone? Was that why a temporary engagement had come to his mind so quickly?

"Listen, let's talk about this at your place. There is a lot more to it than it probably seems to you and I can't explain while I'm driving," he said.

"Sure," she said, turning to stare out the window at the passing scenery. All her life she'd lost herself in books. Ignored some things in her family that were less than ideal because she created a world for herself that involved the stories she read. She admitted it had been very nice. And at the age of thirty-nine, she'd finally created a reality around her where she didn't have to escape into those fictional worlds as often as she'd used to. But this baby and this engagement—they were rocking her real world. Shaking her reality and making her realize that perhaps she hadn't come as far as she'd thought.

When Slade pulled into the guest parking lot, she was relieved because he didn't plan to stay overnight. But when they approached her building, there was a small gathering of paparazzi waiting. She almost wanted to groan, but Slade just pulled her close, wrapping his arm around her shoulders as he led her past them.

Which just confused her more.

He did care for her. He was probably the last man who wanted to be close to the scandal that was surrounding her and her family at the moment, but he was still here. Of course, he was very good at ignoring the rumors and rising above them.

Though she had known that from the first time they'd slept together, this kind of gesture wasn't what anyone in the media would expect from him.

"Fellas," he said, nodding toward the paparazzi as the doorman held open the door and they walked past.

* * *

No one would ever call him a genius, but he was definitely picking up what Melinda was putting down. She looked pissed. The kind of pissed that was going to take a lot more than a Conti heirloom ring and some smooth talking to get around. He didn't blame her one bit. Her life was a mess and he was the one at the center of it.

Though to be fair, her father was doing his part as well. But her dad wasn't here. Slade was and he needed to figure out how to make this right. If he were a different man, he'd be doing everything he could to marry her.

A part of him knew that if he could make the engagement real, if he'd marry her and raise the baby together, that would do it. But he couldn't. He had ghosts in his past and that was saying something given that everyone in Houston and probably beyond knew he was the son of an alleged mobster. And Melinda deserved better.

She didn't offer him a drink when they entered her condo, just walked into the living room and sat down on the large armchair that faced the door. The windows behind her twinkled with the lights of downtown Houston and he had a real impression of how much he was costing her.

Until this moment, it hadn't even occurred to him what the price would be to her if anyone found out they were dating. As she sat there, though, with what used to be her city behind her, it couldn't be clearer.

And he was worried about how he was going to get back into her good graces for the next three months. How was she going to cope with the rest of her life?

"I screwed up," he said. The words were raw and ripped from the most honest place in his soul. The one that knew that he was one step away from following in his criminal father's footsteps. The one that never used the word *alleged* to refer to his dad's activities. Sure, he could put on the polish and look like a Conti when required, but even Nonna knew that the reason Conti Enterprises had flourished under his leadership was that he was a Bartelli through and through. He was the kind of man who never took no for an answer and got what he wanted.

He wanted Melinda. On his terms.

And if he needed further proof that he wasn't the right sort of man to marry and settle down, he'd gotten it. He'd charmed and seduced her until she was in his bed and then the Bartelli luck had kicked in and made a shit hole of her life. He had no way to fix this.

The smart thing to do would be to walk out her front door and find some respectable guy to be the "father" of her kid. But even as the thought entered his mind, he felt a rage welling up inside of him. She belonged to him. The child was his.

He turned away and took several deep breaths. She was her own woman. Not his. But damn. It was hard to accept that.

"You did screw up. But mainly I blame myself because I thought... I should have known better than to trust Philomena. I thought we were friends, but she has told me more than once that blood is thicker than water."

"I know she thinks of you as family—"

"Spare me. I found out the hard way that isn't the truth. And I'm really not in the mood to be placated," she said.

"Fair enough."

She bit her lower lip and looked away from him, staring past his shoulder as she blinked a few times, and he died a little inside because he knew she'd been hoping—maybe not believing, but hoping—that he'd turn out to be a stand-up guy.

"I'm so sorry," he said, quietly.

She nodded. "Of course. Now let's get all our cards on the table. You know where I stand. Pregnant, reputation in tatters. What about you? Temporarily engaged or really engaged to make your nonna happy? Wants a family, doesn't want a family?"

He hesitated. The truth was more complex than he wanted to share with her, but at this point, his only chance of salvaging any relationship with her was to come clean. But that part of himself... He had never wanted her to know about it.

But now it wasn't as if she could think any lower of him than she did at that moment.

He moved into the living room and sat down at the hassock by her feet and looked up at her.

"I guess I should start with Nonna. She wants me to settle down with a woman who could be a partner to me. She wants great-grandchildren and to be honest, she adores you. She suggested I take her spot on the art council to meet you. But the truth is, once I met you, I couldn't help asking you out."

"Why?" she asked.

He had never been one of those men who could easily verbalize his feelings. That wasn't the kind of man he was; but as he looked at Melinda, he knew he had to give her something. She wasn't the kind of woman who did temporary. There was a reason she had never married and it wasn't because men hadn't asked her before. She was selective about who she let into her inner circle.

And she'd let him in.

"In that art council meeting, you were funny while the chair was speaking. All of those little comments under your breath. I was intrigued and then when you got up to talk about Salvador Dalí and why we should sponsor the exhibit..." He couldn't tell her he'd gotten turned on just hearing her passion for the artist. "I knew I wanted to go out with you."

"I turned you down," she reminded him.

"You did. But I haven't gotten to where I am in life by letting a setback affect me. I knew eventually you'd start seeing Slade and not just a Bartelli."

She leaned over, touching his hand. "You were never just a Bartelli to me. But tonight I realized you might have more of your father's traits than I had anticipated."

"Sarcasm really doesn't suit you," he said gently. "I've apologized."

"I know. I'm hurt... Look, maybe we shouldn't do this tonight," she said.

"I think we have to. Let's get it settled so that tomorrow we can start fresh."

She put her arms around her waist and shifted deeper into the chair. "Okay. Go on."

"So Nonna was satisfied and tonight when we told her about the engagement, she was over the moon, but our agreement hasn't changed," he said.

"Why not?"

He took a deep breath. This was harder than he thought it would be.

"Do you mind if I get a drink? This isn't going to be easy to talk about."

"Sure... Go ahead and help yourself."

He came back and instead of sitting down near her, he stood next to her chair facing the floor-to-ceiling windows that overlooked downtown Houston. She loved the view normally. Liked looking down at the city she loved and seeing it from up here. But as she glanced over at Slade, she didn't feel the same kind of peace or satisfaction she normally felt.

She was still mad, so she was trying not to let herself empathize with him. He'd indicated whatever else he had to tell was going to be difficult to hear.

She shook her head.

She had known a tight ass and a pair of bedroom eyes would be her downfall, but she'd never realized how far she had to fall. But he was more than a hot bod to burn up the sheets with. She liked the way he listened to her when she talked about her projects and how he'd sometimes text her during the day when he saw something that he thought she'd like.

Last week, it had been a brown-eyed Susan flower that had somehow grown up between the cracked sidewalk outside one of the Conti warehouses. Those gestures made it very difficult for her to see him as someone with a dark past.

She heard the rattle of the ice in his lowball glass as he took a sip of the whiskey he'd poured for himself. He wasn't a sophisticated drinker and even though her bar was fully stocked, he always went for Johnnie Walker.

"Okay. Say what you have to say," she said. A part of her wanted him out of the condo, so she could regroup and figure out what was next. Angela was used to dealing with scandal and a fiancé their father didn't like. Maybe she could help Melinda figure this out. But Ryder loved Angela… That was one thing Melinda couldn't say about Slade.

She couldn't just walk away from him, because the party tonight had been full of Houston society elite. Everyone had seen them together as a couple, which was what they'd wanted until she found out… what? That he'd used her? Well, get in line, right? Her dad had been doing it for years if rumors were to be believed. Using her good work to cover his own shady dealings.

She'd about had it with the men in her life.

"Um, it's not… That is to say—"

"Stop. Just say it. Does it have to do with your father? I know you're associated with the Bartelli… What do they call it? Syndicate? Mob? Gang?"

"He calls it the family," Slade said.

"The family," she repeated. That had to make it harder for Slade to walk away from. She glanced over at him, standing so alone and stiff and staring out the window.

Despite her anger, she did feel the stirring of sympathy for him. He had grown up in such an odd world. High-society half the time, street-level crime the other.

"Yeah, this might seem like more than you want to know, but I feel like you will just think I'm the biggest douchebag in the world unless you know the whole thing," he said on a heavy sigh as he moved over to the couch and sat down facing toward her.

He had his legs spread and put his forearms on both of his legs. He had left his tie and jacket on, so he still looked like the cover of a *GQ* magazine, but in his eyes, she saw the steel that made Slade the man he was today.

"I'm listening."

And she was. She'd heard the rumors about the Bartelli family, and she knew that despite the fact that everyone said "alleged," they were not a family to be crossed.

"My mom was a bit of a rebel to hear Nonna tell it and her father was very strict. So when Carlo Bartelli flirted with her, she went after him with everything she had. I guess he was dangerous, and she liked that for a while, but her goal had been to piss the old man off. So once her dad was paying attention again, she went back to her regular life and then found out she was pregnant with me."

Melinda had never in her life sympathized with another person as much as she did with Slade's mom in that moment. Though she'd been older and more mature and should have known better, she totally understood what it was like to fall under the spell of a Bartelli.

"But her old man wasn't about to let her have a kid without being married and I think that Nonno honestly thought that he'd be able to bring Carlo around to his way of thinking. Make him legit and part of the Conti family," Slade said.

But he hadn't. That had to have been hard on everyone. The Conti family was old money and had been a part of Houston society since the early 1900s.

"What happened?"

"They got married, got a nice house in River Oaks down the street from my grandparents and until I was eight, everyone thought that Carlo had turned over a new leaf. He worked for Conti Enterprises, he went to the social engagements with my mom and he was a pretty good dad to me. But then he was arrested, and the truth started trickling out. He had never let go of his old life and had been living two lives. Getting caught and having his lawyer get him off on the charges, while the *Houston Chronicle* society pages painted it all as a misunderstanding. You see, my grandmother had a lot of influence back in those days. But Mom knew the truth and my parents separated.

"My dad said there was no way he could get out of the Bartelli family. There just wasn't a way to separate it from the man he was. I thought that was just his weakness and told him so. But I was engaged when I was twenty-one, Melinda. And the Bartellis were at war with another gang and she... Well, she got caught in the middle and was used as a bargaining chip against me. She was okay physically but after that...she didn't want a relationship with me. And I promised myself I'd never put a woman in that position again."

Melinda hadn't realized he'd been engaged but honestly, she hadn't researched him at all. Just took him at face value. That was more her style. And her gut said that his few sentences about what happened were the cleaned-up version.

"Okay. So, we stick to our original plan?"

"Yes. I will protect you and our child forever, but I can never marry you unless I want to give my father's enemies someone to go after. We will be engaged for three months and then reassess and keep pushing the date back until we know the scandal has passed."

Eight

It wasn't as if anything he said surprised her. She knew he'd come from a tough background. To be perfectly honest, that was what had drawn her to him. He was polished at times, but there was always an edginess to him that drew her like a moth to a flame.

"I didn't know you'd been engaged," she said at last.

"Not many people did. I wasn't the CEO of Conti back then. I was just on the fringes of society, some punk kid that might be joining the Bartelli family business. And despite how everyone acted toward me tonight, it took a while for polite society to warm up to me being at events," he admitted.

"I can understand that. I mean, my family is part

of the Texas Cattleman's Club in Royal and the new one opening here in Houston and it is hard to become a member. It wasn't that long ago when it was men only."

"I bet you didn't stand for that," he said with a wry smile.

"Not at all. But I was here in Houston and not really part of the group who was pushing for membership," she admitted. "What are we going to do?"

"Well, I told you we'll do the engagement for three months like we agreed and then hopefully media interest in you will have died down enough that you can get back to your old routine."

She shifted in the chair, wishing she'd worn pumps instead of sandals with an ankle strap so she could just kick them off, but she hadn't, so she crossed her legs and sat up straighter. "What about the baby?"

"I'll provide you with everything you need. Money, furniture… I'll even pay for the child's tuition to the best schools in Houston."

"Thanks, but I'm not asking about money," she said. "What about you? Will you be a part of the child's life?"

"No. I'm not role-model material," he said. He took another swallow of his whiskey, finishing it and leaning forward to place the glass on the coffee table.

"Why not? Do you really not like me?"

"FAST FIVE" READER SURVEY

Your participation entitles you to:
✳ **4 Thank-You Gifts Worth Over \$20!**

Complete the survey in minutes.

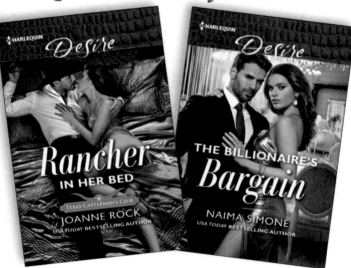

Get **2 FREE** Books

Your Thank-You Gifts include **2 FREE BOOKS** and **2 MYSTERY GIFTS**. There's no obligation to purchase anything!

See inside for details.

Dear Reader,

Since you are a lover of our books, your opinions are important to us... and so is your time.

That's why we made sure your **"FAST FIVE" READER SURVEY** can be completed in just a few minutes. Your answers to the five questions will help us remain at the forefront of women's fiction.

And, as a thank-you for participating, we'd like to send you **4 FREE THANK-YOU GIFTS!**

Enjoy your gifts with our appreciation,

Pam Powers

To get your
4 FREE THANK-YOU GIFTS:

✷ Quickly complete the "Fast Five" Reader Survey
and return the insert.

"FAST FIVE" READER SURVEY

1 Do you sometimes read a book a second or third time? ○ Yes ○ No

2 Do you often choose reading over other forms of entertainment such as television? ○ Yes ○ No

3 When you were a child, did someone regularly read aloud to you? ○ Yes ○ No

4 Do you sometimes take a book with you when you travel outside the home? ○ Yes ○ No

5 In addition to books, do you regularly read newspapers and magazines? ○ Yes ○ No

YES! I have completed the above Reader Survey. Please send me my 4 FREE GIFTS (gifts worth over $20 retail). I understand that I am under no obligation to buy anything, as explained on the back of this card.

225/326 HDL GNQC

FIRST NAME

LAST NAME

ADDRESS

APT.#

CITY

STATE/PROV.

ZIP/POSTAL CODE

"Hell, woman, you know I like you. You wouldn't be pregnant if I didn't," he blurted.

But that bluster didn't really bother her. She knew he was being defensive, but for the life of her, she couldn't figure out why.

"So what is it, then?" she asked.

He tipped his head to the side, studying her for a moment. "Not even a rebuke for the way I spoke to you?"

"I know you well enough to tell when you're lashing out to hide something," she said.

"We do know each other fairly well now, don't we?"

She noticed he was still not answering her question. Interesting. They did know each other well. She'd thought they were falling in love. But Slade wasn't that kind of man, she guessed.

"I would have thought so, but then I learned tonight that we were set up by Philomena…"

Right now, she wanted to get to the bottom of why Slade didn't want to raise a child. He wasn't just averse to making a home and having a family, he was talking about no contact with the child at all.

Why?

"So back to the child…" she continued.

"Please. Will you let it go?" he asked. "Just for tonight."

There was something raw in the way he asked, and she found that she couldn't force anything else. Her mind was already full of everything that had gone on today and maybe it was time to just let the day end.

"Okay, but I'm going to want some answers eventually," she said.

"Fair enough," he said, standing up. "I guess I should be going…"

Of course, she wanted him to stay. She was tired and if she were being completely honest, more than a little scared about being a mom at forty. But there were too many dangers if she let him stay.

Tonight had made it clear how complicated this entire situation was. If there was ever a time when she needed a clear head, it was now. She couldn't afford to let herself get used to Slade. That meant sleeping with him wasn't going to happen.

Again.

"Yes, I think you should be," she said.

"Fair enough," he said, standing up, and she did the same. He came over to her and pulled her into his arms and she noticed how easy it was to rest her head on his chest right over his heart.

She heard the sound of it beating under her ear as he held her close, rubbing his hands up and down her back.

"I'm sorry for all of this," he said. "I think that just goes to show how stupid I can be at times."

She smiled because he couldn't see it. He always surprised her. He was so aware of his faults and never hesitated to try to make amends for them. It was why she didn't understand his reluctance to be a father to their child. Surely whatever was in his past, he could overcome it.

She tipped her head back to look up at him. Their eyes met and she saw the hunger and need in his gaze. It mirrored the feelings churning inside of her. She knew it would be smarter to send him away. But she also knew by the end of the year, Slade would be out of her life. The man she'd waited forever for was only here for a few more months.

Could she take what she wanted and still be whole when it ended?

Leaving was the last thing he wanted to do. He wanted to hold her. Just hold her and for a moment forget that he'd been born a Bartelli.

Forget that his uncles and extended goombahs weren't ever going to let a child of his walk away the way he had.

"Slade, I know what I said earlier but do you want to stay the night?" she asked. Her voice was soft and entreating, and she put her hand on his face like she did sometimes. It always made it impossible for him to say no to her.

"I'd like nothing more," he admitted. "But you have to know—"

She put her fingers over his lips to stop the words that would have warned her about him and his family, and he let her because the last thing he wanted to do was tell her what a mess his family was.

"No more talking," she said. "We both know the facts but tonight is for us. Just you and me...and our new child."

He had to smile at the way she said it. He wasn't a man given to wishing, but at this moment, he longed to be anyone but Slade Bartelli. It didn't matter that he knew in his gut he never would have met her if he weren't himself.

He wrapped his arm around her waist, lifting her off her feet, and carried her toward the stairs that led to her bedroom. She wrapped her arm around his shoulders and put one hand on his chest as she loosened his tie. After this day, which had felt like a lifetime, he needed this. Needed her in a way that he never would want to admit to another soul, but she did something to him that went beyond sex.

Maybe that explained that feeling he'd had when Nonna had said what she had about pushing him to meet her. As if he needed an incentive other than Melinda to ask her out.

He kissed her then. He couldn't wait another moment because he felt like she was slipping away from him. That he'd lost his chance to keep her... Wait, he wasn't keeping her. This was just for tonight.

Her tongue rubbed over his and everything masculine inside of him went on red alert. He wanted to take her in the hallway up against the wall. Just take her hard and deep until there was no doubt that she was his. That she belonged to him...with him. No matter what logic said, his instincts demanded he make Melinda his.

Pixie danced around his feet as he entered Melinda's bedroom. The little dog stood on her back legs and he realized she might need to go out. Maybe they were never going to have sex again, he thought. Between the paparazzi, his family, her family and now her dog, it seemed as if the cards were stacked against them.

He set Melinda on her feet. A tendril of hair had escaped her updo and fell against the side of her face. He touched her check, brushing it back behind her ear. She was so beautiful that she took his breath away.

Pixie let out a small bark.

"Does she need to go out?" he asked.

"She should be okay," Melinda said. "Let me check."

Melinda opened the door that led to her outdoor balcony, which ran the length of her condo. She had a small grassy "lawn" area that she'd had installed just for her dog. Pixie didn't like the noise on the streets and the nervous dog would often start shaking.

He followed Melinda to the glass door. As soon as she opened it, the little dog darted out and the warm September air rushed into the room. Slade took off his tie and loosened his collar. He tossed his tie on the chair and then toed off his shoes and socks.

Melinda braced one hand on the doorjamb and bent to undo the buckle at her ankle on her sandals. He hardened watching her body move, so graceful and elegant. When she glanced over at him, finding him watching her, there was a heat in her eyes. He groaned.

She always met him heat for heat. He had expected a shy woman in the bedroom given her propensity for manners and rules, but she knew what she wanted from a man and didn't hesitate to demand it. Something he appreciated in her.

There was a lot about Melinda that had kept him coming back to her bedroom. He'd never admit it out loud, but he regretted the baby she was carrying. That child was forcing him out of her life. Yet at the same time, he was intensely protective of that child. The baby that shouldn't have been because he'd made a vow to himself. Of course, he'd broken it. Did he need further proof that he was a Bartelli?

He had it. No more thinking. He wanted Melinda in his arms and underneath him. At least then he'd feel like he was giving her what she needed from him. And when he held her, he could pretend even for a few moments that she was his.

Really his.

She got her shoes off and stood there across from

him, looking sexier than anyone he'd ever seen before. She wasn't even doing anything to tempt him, just being Melinda, and honestly that was all that it took. He walked toward her, catching her in his arms and pulling her more fully against him, so that they were pressed together from chest to pelvis. He kissed her slowly, thoroughly and very deeply. He caught her earlobe between his teeth.

"I need you now," he said.

"Here?" she asked, but it was what she wanted and needed as well. There was something about Slade that made her forget all her normal rules of behavior. He called to something wild inside of her.

The city of Houston was spread out behind them, but she wanted him. She walked over to the glass doors and glanced at her dog as she played in her yard area. Slade came up behind her and slowly drew the zipper down the side of her dress and she shivered as his finger brushed against her side.

"Right here," he said, as he lifted the back of her dress up until she felt the brush of his trousers against the back of her legs.

He reached down and traced the fabric of her thong, his finger running on the edge of her crack and making her hips arch instinctively.

She put one hand on the glass door in front of them, as she heard him lowering his zipper and then felt the heat of him against her. His erection rubbed against her backside as he held her to him with his hand on her stomach.

She arched back against him as he kissed the column of her neck and sucked against the point where it met her shoulder.

His hands moved along her stomach and lower, pushing her underwear down her body and she worked them down to her feet. She pushed her hips back as she stepped out of them, her backside rubbing against his erection. He groaned and clenched her waist.

He put his hands over hers on the glass, lacing their fingers together as she felt him thrusting against her. He shifted his hips back until the tip of his erection was at the entrance of her body. She bit her lower lip as he entered her slowly, her head falling back against his shoulder, turning until their lips met.

He sucked her tongue into his mouth as he drove deep inside her. She moaned, arching against him to take him deeper, and he held her tightly to him with his hand on her stomach as he drove himself in and out of her body.

She felt so close to coming but wanted to draw this out and make it last. But really, could anything with Slade Bartelli last? She knew it was fleeting. Full of more emotion than she'd ever experienced before and probably something she'd miss for the rest of life once he walked out of it.

Tears burned her eyes and she ripped her mouth

from his, turning her head away from him. In the reflection of the glass, she caught a glimpse of him and was dazzled by the intensity in his gaze as he moved in and out of her body. When their eyes met, she saw so much in him that she wanted to see. Wanted to believe.

Before she could finish the thought, his hand on her stomach moved lower. He rubbed her clit just the way she liked it and she felt herself tightening around him and then her climax burst through her. Spots danced in front of her eyes and she closed them as he thrust harder and faster into her until he came, calling her name. His head was buried in her back between her shoulder blades and he held her so tightly. She wanted him to keep holding her this way. To never let her go. But that wasn't possible.

He turned her in his arms, putting his hand under her chin and tipping her head back. She felt the tears stir again, knew it was because the sex had been so good. She wanted to make herself believe that he was going to stay. That he was going to be her man not just for these few more weeks but forever.

He brushed the tears away with his thumbs.

"Aw, baby cakes, don't cry."

She nodded and put her face in his chest against the fabric of his shirt, but as he rubbed her back, the tears continued to fall. She had to start being real with herself about Slade Bartelli.

She loved him.

She had been pretending that wasn't the case for a while, but it was. And she wanted him to be her fiancé not to get the paparazzi off their tail but because he wanted to spend the rest of his life with her.

"Every time I try to make things better, I make them worse," he said, his voice full of something close to regret or maybe loathing.

"No. It's not you. You've always been honest with me," she admitted.

"Somehow that isn't making me feel any better," he said. "I hate seeing you like this."

She wanted to be able to laugh and flirt and somehow turn this entire thing around, but she couldn't. It wasn't in her at this moment. All she could do was muster a weak smile as Pixie came running back to the door and she stepped aside, her dress falling back into place as she let the dog back inside.

"Should I leave?" he asked. "Would that make this all better?"

She had no idea. "I am so lost right now, Slade. I can't tell if anything will help. I don't know what to do and for the first time in my life, I'm going to be responsible for another person…a child. I'm just losing it in a way that I never thought I would."

"You're not alone," he said. "I'm here."

"But you won't be for long."

"Can't we just take this as it comes? Live in the moment?"

She wanted to say no. But really, what options

did she have? She loved this man and right now, she wasn't strong enough to tell him she wouldn't settle for the bread crumbs he offered her.

"Yes, let's try that."

He didn't look convinced but spent the rest of the evening doing everything to make her happy. He drew a bath for her, washed her hair and then read to her because he knew she liked the sound of his voice. And she tucked the memory away along with her sadness because she didn't want him to know that when he was sweet to her like this, it made her ache for what could have been.

Nine

Planning a big soiree to announce their engagement was the last thing that Melinda wanted to do. Oh, who was she kidding? It was the exact thing she wanted to do and had been secretly dreaming of for most of her adult life. But she also knew the bigger deal that was made out of the engagement, the harder it was going to be to move on when it was over. Slade had said they'd reassess after three months, but she had also heard the iron in his voice when he said he didn't want to get married.

She wasn't stupid. She knew that she had to keep her head about this, but she couldn't help looking down at the huge rock, the Conti family heirloom, that Slade had slipped on her finger after he'd made love to her last Wednesday night. It was a week later and he'd been good to his word, escorting her to functions and even setting up a romantic lunch with her so that the media would have some photos to run other than that scorching hot kiss they'd shared at the opera…the one that had outed them.

"Earth to Mels… Anyone home?" Angela asked as she handed her a coffee and sat down across from her at the party planners. This kind of engagement announcement party was going to require the big guns and since they were holding it on Saturday, it really didn't give her enough time to do it on her own. Her father hadn't been over the moon at the news, but he liked Slade so he'd offered to foot the bill, which had reassured Melinda that his money troubles were all speculation and rumor.

"I'm trying not to be jealous of the fact that Daddy is so happy about your engagement and is still trying to convince me to break things off with Ryder."

"How is everything going with Ryder?" Melinda asked. "I thought Daddy would soften toward him now that he's out of jail."

"You know Daddy. He's tried, but he really can't seem to stop hating on Ryder," Angela said. "But that's not what we are here today to talk about. How can I help?"

"I'm just trying to figure out how to get this all done," she said.

"You'll do it and it will be the event of the season," Angela said. "You're always good at making your dreams come true."

There was a note of melancholy in her sister's voice. Their father had yet to give his approval of Angela's engagement, even though Ryder was a successful businessman.

"I'm sorry," she said.

"It's not your fault. But if Daddy says one more thing about how Slade is the catch of the century, I might have to remind him Slade's family is a bit… shady."

Her father just said things like that in what Melinda could only guess was the hope that Angela would drop Ryder and find another man, a man that in his eyes was a better one. Though Slade had assured her that he wasn't part of the Bartelli business, it was hard to dodge these kinds of inferences. "He's not like that, Angela."

"I know," her sister said, putting her hand over Melinda's. "I'm sorry, it's just hard to see Dad talking about Slade like he's the perfect future son-in-law and treating Ryder like he's some kind of disease."

She squeezed her sister's hand. She had been so caught up in her own crazy life she hadn't really been there for Angela lately.

"I'm sorry. Slade's not perfect," Melinda said. "I wonder if Dad would come around if we had a double wedding."

"Double wedding?"

"Yes, you know like we used to play when we were little. Remember?" she asked. But even as the words were leaving Melinda's mouth, she wondered if she were going crazy. Ryder and Angela were in love—real love—and about to really get married. She and Slade had some crazy, sexy lust thing between them, a baby that neither of them planned for and a temporary engagement that he had no intention to fulfill.

"You're sweet, but I don't want to intrude on your special day…or mine," Angela said.

"Well, if you change your mind…I don't mind making this about us instead of me," Melinda said. "I'm really not much for the spotlight. And a double wedding might be the thing to change the attitude of the journalists covering Dad's…troubles."

Angela laughed. "It might. I'd only do it if he accepted Ryder and I really can't see that happening anytime soon."

"To be honest, I'm surprised he likes Slade as much as he does. I was worried our relationship might have a negative effect on his legal issues, but the truth is, Slade is so transparent, I think it's actually helping Dad."

"I agree. I mean, his family is shady, but I've been hard-pressed to find anyone who actually believes that Slade is in the business with them."

"Me too," she admitted. "And the Contis are above reproach."

"They are. I think that's what makes him palatable. What does he say about his father's business?" Angela asked.

Nothing. But she didn't want her sister to realize there were things that she hadn't been able to talk to her fiancé about. If Angela told her that Ryder kept things from her, she would caution her sister to push for answers. This was a mess. She put her head down, staring at the red lipstick stain on the lid of her to-go coffee cup.

"What is it?" Angela asked.

What is it? There was so much she wanted to share with Angela, but could she? Could she tell her everything and still carry on doing what she needed to? Absently, she toyed with the heirloom engagement ring on her left hand.

Melinda lifted her head and glanced around. They were still waiting for the party planner to come in and talk to them about Saturday's big party. They were alone in the conference room with the party books spread out in front of them.

"I'm afraid once I tell you, you're going to realize that I'm in over my head."

"What are you talking about?" Angela asked. "What's going on?"

"Well… I'm pregnant," she said.

"Oh, yay! I'm going to be an auntie! You said you wanted to be a mom and now you're going to be," Angela said, hugging her. "I love this. I was starting to think our family was cursed but this baby seems like a blessing."

"It does," Melinda agreed. She could never think of her child as anything but a blessing. "Slade suggested marriage to keep the society bloggers from guessing that it was unplanned."

"That's not what I was expecting, but he's standing by you as he should. How do you feel about that?"

"I want to marry him and have that whole white-picket-fence life, you know me, but I want him to love me too. And Slade has some baggage that makes him think he can't do that."

"I thought he asked you to marry him. He is your fiancé, right?"

Melinda rubbed her thumb over the lipstick mark on the cup. Angela might as well know the entire truth. "Temporarily. He won't marry me or be a father to our child."

Angela knew a lot of things about her twin and the most important was that she'd never agree to a temporary engagement without a plan to make it permanent. Melinda was just doubting herself and since Angela was so happy and in love, she knew she could help Melinda see what she needed to do.

"What are we going to do? Can you change his mind?"

"I don't know. But I said yes because I hope so."

Angela shifted around in the chair and turned

Melinda's to face her as well. She was going to be an auntie. She hugged her sister. "Congrats on the baby. Are you excited about it?"

"I am. I mean, there's so much other stuff that I'm dealing with but when I have a quiet moment, I just think about it. I had pretty much written off being a mom. I was in denial at first. I mean, how could I be pregnant at this age?"

"Forty is the new thirty. I read that someplace, so you know you can believe it."

"Ha. It doesn't feel like the new thirty," she said. When she'd been twenty-nine, she'd felt like she had total control over her life and at this moment, she felt like she was rolling and spinning in a million different directions. She had no idea how to control anything.

"I agree some days it's harder than others to believe that this might be the new thirty, but to be honest, I think I like the attitude it gives me. I mean, Dad and Ryder aren't exactly best buddies, and Dad is still convinced somehow Ryder had something to do with the investigation into him and these murder rumors that are swirling, but I keep hoping both of them will come around eventually. Remember how you had said that no man that we like is inappropriate?"

"I guess I was…I don't know what," Melinda said with a laugh. When she'd been starting to fall for Slade and saw Angela falling for Ryder, she had felt like they could have everything they desired. But it had gotten complicated for both of them.

Angela hugged her close, understanding that Melinda was trying to use humor to mask her fears. "Something drew you to Slade and him to you. And right now, he's saying that he doesn't want to raise a family—why did he ask you to marry him, then?"

Her sister flushed and then bit her lower lip, blinking several times. What the heck was going on with Melinda?

"He did it to protect me from the media. But he made it clear it's only temporary. We're going to distract them with the engagement and then reassess before Christmas."

That was crazy. There was no way a man who looked at her sister the way Slade did was ever going to let her go. No matter what Slade was telling himself.

"I think if he asked you to marry him to protect you, then he's not really thinking it's just for a short time. He has been single all these years," Angela said. "Something about you made him finally commit."

Melinda shook her head. "He doesn't want to disappoint his grandmother either, so I think the engagement is sort of a way to protect me, get the press off our backs and appease her."

"Do you even hear what you're saying? I can't for a moment imagine that Slade Bartelli would give in to that kind of pressure. If I had to guess, I'd say he wants you to force him to make the engagement a real one. Seems to me that he's done everything but say the words to show you that's what he wants."

"Angela, if you had to force Ryder to ask you to marry him, would you? Could you ever be happy, knowing that the only reason you were married was because you got pregnant? I want Slade to marry me because he wants to spend the rest of his life with me. Even when he was confronted with the fact that I knew he'd been influenced to ask me out, he still wouldn't say that he wanted me."

"No, I wouldn't want that," she said, hugging her sister again. This was one of those times when they needed their mom to give them advice, but it was only the two of them. "Oh, honey, I'm sorry. Are you sure?"

Melinda chewed her lower lip between her teeth and just shook her head. "No. There are times when I'm sure that Slade is the perfect man for me. But the truth is until he can come to me and say he wants this to be real, I'm not going to be able to believe it. I can't just act like it's real when it's not. I do feel bad about lying to Philomena. I mean, I'm wearing her great-grandmother's ring and I love it. I want to think it will always be on my hand, but it won't be."

Angela had no real words to comfort her sister.

Her own love life, while happy, was still not perfect because their father hadn't accepted Ryder, but hearing this pain in her sister's voice made her heart break. How could Slade do this to her sister?

"I'm going to talk to him."

"No. You're not. I will figure this out," Melinda said. "I appreciate that you would try to intervene for me, but this is my mess and I'm going to sort it out."

"I don't think you should refer to the father of your child as a mess," Angela said with a smile, trying to tease her sister back into a better a mood.

"I agree, but it's better than calling him an ass," Melinda said with a tiny smile.

"Even if that is what he is," Angela agreed.

"Who's an ass?" their father asked from the doorway. "I hope it's not me."

Angela saw the look on Melinda's face and realized her sister wasn't even close to being able to carry off a temporary engagement. Slade was asking the impossible.

"You can be, Daddy," Melinda said. "But today with both of your daughters engaged, I think we can agree that you're not."

Nothing made Sterling Perry happier than spending time with his children. Now that the fraud charges against him had been dropped, he was ready to get back to his normal life. Enough of being treated like a criminal.

He couldn't be happier that Melinda had finally found a man who could keep up with her and wasn't put off by the walls that his daughter tended to place around herself. Slade might not have been everyone's first choice for a son-in-law, but Sterling knew the man to be shrewd in business and damn hard to intimidate. He was the perfect match for Melinda.

He remembered his own engagement and how happy he'd been. That had been a long time ago. Before things had fallen apart. Jealousy and pride had driven a wedge between them that Sterling had never figured out how to fix. He knew he had his share of the blame and he hoped his daughters fared better in marriage than he had. But both of them seemed to be making choices…that were going to make their situations harder.

"What do you think of this?" Melinda asked, smiling over at him with her blue eyes so full of happiness that he couldn't help smiling back. He loved seeing that joy on her face. Slade did seem to genuinely care about his daughter and the man made her happy, what more could a father want?

"I'm sorry, Mels, I wasn't paying attention. What is this for again?" he asked.

She laughed. "It's for the table linens."

He shook his head. "Why don't I leave my credit card and let you two handle the rest of the details."

"Sounds good, since you've never really cared about these kinds of details," Angela said.

He wasn't sure if there was an edge to her tone or if he was imagining it because she knew he didn't like Ryder. He wanted his daughters to be happy, but Sterling could never trust Ryder.

He kissed both of his daughters on their foreheads and left them to sort out the party details. He gave his credit card information to the receptionist and then stepped out into the hot Houston afternoon. He glanced at his cell phone and saw that some of his longtime investors were still messaging him to be reassured that they hadn't been set up in a Ponzi scheme.

Damn that Ryder Currin. He had made it look like all of Sterling's legitimate investments were questionable. What would it take for Angela to be free of Ryder once and for all?

He walked to his car when the idea hit him. Perhaps Ryder needed a taste of his own medicine. If Ryder's precious Currin Oil were to be engulfed in a cloud of suspicion, maybe Angela would wake up and find herself a better man.

All it had taken for the investigation to be started into Sterlings's dealings was an anonymous tip. Something he had long suspected that Ryder Currin had a hand in. The more he thought about it, the angrier it made him. And while he knew he should be happy the charges were dropped, thanks to his lawyer son, Roarke, Sterling hadn't enjoyed having the negative publicity surround him and his company. The Perrys had been in Texas for a long time and had always been upstanding citizens.

He couldn't help but believe that Ryder was behind him being questioned in regard to Vincent Hamm's murder too.

Sterling had always been an Old Testament kind of man. Eye-for-an-eye sounded about right to him.

He couldn't make the call, but there was no reason one of his staff couldn't raise a legitimate concern.

He drove through the afternoon traffic and when he was back in his office, he called for one of his staffers.

He remembered the way that Angela had looked when he'd walked out of the party planner's office. She wasn't happy with him. She wanted him to accept the man she loved. But how could he? Ryder was everything he didn't want in his family.

He rubbed the back of his neck. Throwing a man's business into jeopardy... That wasn't his way. He didn't want to cost good men their jobs, only bring Ryder to the attention of law enforcement and cause him the same kind of problems that he'd created for Sterling. And maybe, please, God, Angela would come to her senses and leave Ryder.

"I heard some rather disturbing news today and it's the kind of thing that needs to be brought to the attention of the labor board. But because of my personal involvement I'd rather someone else handled it," Sterling said.

"What is it about?" his second assistant asked.

"It's about unfair labor practices at the Currin Oil refinery. Now, because of my daughter I wouldn't feel right about saying anything but we both know that labor practices aren't something we can look the other way on," Sterling said.

"I agree. Can you give me a few more details?" his assistant asked.

Sterling outlined the details of the complaint he wanted made against Currin Oil and his assistant looked properly shocked as he took notes, nodding and then reluctantly agreeing.

"I'll call from my office and make the anonymous tip to the labor line. I think you're doing the right thing here, Mr. Perry. Even if he is your daughter's fiancé. That kind of treatment of workers can't be tolerated."

"No, it can't," Sterling agreed as his assistant left his office. He had put up with a lot of crap over the last few weeks, but letting his daughter marry Currin wasn't something he would tolerate and he would do whatever he had to in order to protect her. For as long as he could remember, he'd hated Ryder Currin because he seemed to have some kind of spell over the women that Sterling loved. First, his wife, and now, one of his daughters.

He leaned back in his chair. "You're going down, Currin."

Ten

Ryder Currin was everything that Angela always wanted and never thought she'd have. The fact that he'd finally put a ring on her finger she thought would be the beginning to her happily-ever-after. But nothing ever went that easily for her. Her sister's comment about a double wedding and then bombshell of the truth behind her own engagement had left Angela with a few, well, concerns. Three days after she and her sister had been planning a reception for Melinda's engagement, she decided to go and talk to Ryder about finally setting a wedding date.

Ryder had asked her to marry him, but he'd been

stonewalling her about setting a date and some of the things her father had said made her wonder if he was using her. She wished her dad and Ryder could find a way to get along.

If there was one thing that Angela Perry wasn't, it was a pushover. She strode into the offices of Currin Oil, well aware that the men she passed all stopped to watch her. She enjoyed it and had dressed specifically so she looked her best.

Ryder was on the phone when she walked in and the expression on his face had her stopping in her tracks. He was angry. Angrier than she'd ever seen him before and that was saying something.

He glanced up and his face softened for a moment as he motioned for her to come in and close the door behind her.

She did, but stayed next to the closed door. Whatever was going on with his business seemed like it was pretty intense. She wanted to get a wedding date on the calendar but even she could tell that maybe this wasn't the best time.

Still, she'd come this far, had given herself a pep talk and was determined to find out if she and Melinda were in the same boat. Was Ryder really going to marry her?

He slammed the phone down with more force than was necessary and she had to admit that was one thing she didn't like about her cell phone. There was no way to angrily punch the disconnect button that satisfied the way slamming down the handset on a landline did.

"Sorry, sweetheart. I didn't realize you'd be stopping by today," he said, standing up and coming over to give her a kiss. He took her hand and led her to the seating area in his office. "Can I get you a drink?"

"No, I'm good. Are you okay? You looked like you were ready to kill someone when I walked into the room," she said.

"Not kill, but I'm not in the best mood. Why did you stop by?" he asked.

She smiled weakly but he was watching her and now that she was here, she realized that coming by his office might not have been the best idea. But he'd been dodging talking about them and she needed some reassurance.

"I wanted to discuss the wedding plans. I thought it might take your mind off all that's been going on here. And really all I need your input on is the date. I can take care of the rest."

"Angela." He stood up and walked away, but in the way he said her name, she felt his frustration with her.

"What?" she asked, getting up to follow him. "You asked me to marry you and now you won't set a date or even talk about a possible date. Why is that? Do you really intend to marry me or was this all some kind of plot to get back at my dad?"

He turned to face her, and she saw that anger but also a little bit of what she thought might be hurt in his eyes. "If you think that, then why did you say yes?"

"I love you, Ryder, that's why I said yes. It's not like I'm playing a game with you. I just want to know that we are planning our wedding," she said.

"I get that, babe, but the truth is I can't right now. Someone has leveled accusations of employee mistreatment against the company. I'm trying to investigate that and see if there is any merit to the accusation, because until now I thought I ran a pretty clean company. And I'm pretty sure your father had something to do with the accusation."

She shook her head. "Listen, he might not like you, but he wouldn't stoop to sabotaging your business."

"You really think so? Because I'm pretty sure you thought I had something to do with the allegations against your father."

"I don't understand you two," she said. "And I never said that you had anything to do with that mess, which is all cleared up by the way so it's old news."

But it wasn't. Her father really did believe that Ryder had been the source of his legal troubles and it hadn't made it any easier to try to get him on board with accepting her fiancé. She had to do something. Right now. "We should elope. Just run away—"

"No. You're not listening to me. This isn't some

accusation I can ignore and it will go away. This could cost me everything. I have to find out if there is any truth to the claims and then fix this. I can't run off and get married and pretend everything is okay, or that my daddy will swoop in and fix it. I'm the only one who can do this."

"You're being an ass and I don't like it. You know I don't wait for Dad to save me. I just was thinking that together as a team we would be able to fight this better. But if you want to do it on your own, then—"

She broke off and turned toward the door, but he caught her around the waist, pulling her back into his arms. He hugged her and put his head in the crook of her neck, kissing her. "I'm sorry. It's not you. It's my company. I've invested so much of my life in it and I hate that it's in jeopardy."

"Then let me help you," she said, turning in his arms and kissing him. If it was her father stirring up this trouble, then she would confront him and get to the bottom of it. Helping Ryder figure out what was going on was the least she could do.

Ryder did love her, and she was going to help him figure out this newest obstacle so they could move forward with their lives together.

Ryder had always had a hot temper and most of the time he could control it, but right now it seemed like everything was falling to pieces. He had the woman he loved in his arms, but he couldn't relax. He knew that her father hated him… Nothing new there. He had always been the kind of man that fathers didn't want their daughters dating. Except he was a successful oil tycoon now and not the wildcatter he'd once been. Even he had to admit he scarcely resembled the rough boy of his past.

But that didn't mean that life had suddenly gotten any easier for him. In fact, there were days when he wished he were still a wildcatter who settled things with his fists.

That didn't excuse his lashing out at Angela. It was simply that he couldn't plan for a future when his livelihood was being threatened. And he'd just heard that one of his executives, Willem Inwood, had some questionable practices with the employees and was a terrible manager.

It could all be allegations, but the call he'd just ended made it seem like there was more than a little truth to them. Angela wanted to help, but how could she? And he didn't want to lose her. He needed her by his side.

"We are stronger as a couple," he admitted, lifting her up in his arms, and she wrapped her legs around his hips as their lips met. Damn, it would be easy to distract her and himself with sex, but his office door was unlocked and one of his assistants was coming to talk about Inwood.

"I'm sorry for how I was. I'm just in a piss-poor

mood," he said, carrying her back over to the sofa and sitting down with her on his lap. "Seeing you has made my day better."

"Good, I'm glad to hear that," she said, wrapping her arms around him. "But I can do more than help you feel better. Want me to go do some investigating into the allegations?"

He took a deep breath and then nodded. He was too used to going it alone because for most of his life, the only one he had counted on was himself. But Angela was here, and she wanted to help. "I'm not sure you'll get any further than I did with the complaints officer. He said the tip was anonymous and it was only when he started talking to my employees that he found the accusation had any substance."

"Which employees? I don't think my father could get to them," she said. "The last person your employees would speak to is him."

"I agree, but he might have overheard some grumblings and called the tip in. But he isn't the source of the problems," Ryder admitted. As much as he wanted to blame Sterling, it seemed that one of his executives was at the root of the issue. Which pissed him off. He trusted his employees. When he hired someone to work at Currin Oil he always thought of them as part of his extended family. Now he wondered if that was a mistake.

There was a knock on his office door and Angela

shifted off his lap to sit on the couch as he went to open the door. His assistant was standing there with her tablet in one hand and a stack of files tucked into the curve of her arm.

"I have all the files and there is definitely some cause for alarm—" She stopped talking when she noticed Angela.

"It's okay, Mary. Angela is going to try to help us out here. She has some connections at town hall and so she'll be asking some questions to help us get to the bottom of this."

"Great. I think we're going to need all the help we can get. I can't find Willem. It's almost as if he's just disappeared. I don't want to get the police involved unless we have to. But he might have skipped town."

Well, that looked damned suspicious. He would have liked it better if Willem had come in and denied everything. Or the man could admit to it, then Ryder would know what he was dealing with. Instead, the guy seemed to have taken the coward's way out. "Okay. I have a guy who does investigations for the firm. I'll ask him to try to track down Willem. In the meantime, tell me what you have on the complaints."

"Who is Willem?" Angela asked him.

"Willem Inwood," Ryder said, wrapping his arm around her as she came over to the conference table where Mary had spread out the employee files.

"That name sounds familiar. Have I met him at one of your functions?" she asked.

"I don't think so," Ryder said. "Do you know him from somewhere else?"

"I might. It's like a name from a long time ago," she said. "I'll figure it out. I don't think Daddy knows him but maybe he does."

"I hope not because that would feed into my suspicions of corporate sabotage," he replied. "But I'm sure you'll figure out how you know the name."

"I don't know that I should be looking at any employee files. Can you give me some information about the complaints? Then I'll go and see what kind of information I can dig up," she said.

Mary handed her a copy of the formal complaint, which Angela read. "Okay, let me see what I can find out."

"Thanks, babe," Ryder said, walking her to his office door and stepping out into the hallway with her. It was clear and he pulled her into his arms, kissing her again. "I am sorry about earlier. You mean the world to me, and once I get this sorted, we can start planning the wedding of your dreams."

"I want it to be the wedding of *our* dreams," she said, going up on tiptoe and kissing him before she turned and walked away.

All of his dreams were just to have the woman he loved by his side.

* * *

Melinda decided she'd had enough of everything and everyone and a trip to the Red Door Salon was what she needed to get herself back on track. She texted Angela to see if she wanted to meet her for an afternoon at the spa.

Angela had one more thing to do but she'd meet her around three o'clock.

Melinda decided to go early and get her hair trimmed.

Melinda's assistant was waiting for her when she came into her office at the foundation she co-founded with her sorority sister. She handed Pixie to Alfie. "I booked her a grooming appointment. Do you mind running her over?"

"Not at all," he replied. He handed her a stack of messages. "As you can see, we've had a few more media requests. Have you and Slade set a wedding date?" Alfie asked. "I'm thinking that would appease them for now."

A wedding date? For their big day? No, they hadn't set one and she knew they never would and that was kind of what pushed her over the edge. How was she supposed to do this? No one wanted to spend his or her entire life in one big lie…or rather, she didn't. She was really upset that Slade had put her in this position. Sure, she understood… No, actually she didn't understand why he couldn't just marry her.

Other than the fact that no matter how he tried to frame it, he didn't love her. And he didn't want to spend the rest of his life with her.

"I don't have a date, Alfie. But for now, tell them we're planning a big engagement party for Saturday the twenty-first. We will be inviting a limited number of social bloggers and reporters," she said. "And if you don't mind, make a list of those bloggers who you think will treat us kindly and not like some kind of salacious episode of a reality TV show."

"I'll do that. Come on, Miss Pixie," Alfie said, tapping his leg, and the dachshund followed him out of her office.

Alfie closed the door behind him, and Melinda walked over to her desk and sat on the edge of it. Right now, she had been running from fire to fire and trying to stay ahead of the blaze, but it wasn't working. She needed to dig a trench like those firefighters did when a blaze was out of control…or call in reinforcements. The only problem was she had no reinforcements.

Angela had said she needed to listen to her own advice when it came to Slade, and Melinda realized that she was afraid to do that. Afraid to admit that after all these years of waiting for Mr. Right, she'd made Slade into something he wasn't.

He had completely rocked her world and what they had together in bed was like nothing she'd ever imagined. She'd definitely believed sex was over-rated until she'd done it with him. But there was more to relationships than sex.

Slade looked good in a tux and in a pair of faded jeans, but clothes didn't always make the man. She knew that. So was she seeing something in Slade that wasn't there?

Was she being naive because a part of her acknowledged that if she were ever going to settle down, this was definitely the time to do it?

Or was it that positive pregnancy test that had her convinced they had to be in love?

She'd had feelings for Slade for a while now. She'd been afraid to admit them because he clearly wasn't looking for marriage with her or, to be fair, with any woman.

And the baby... She touched her stomach not because she felt maternal but because she felt like she might be sick. She wasn't ready for a child. She still felt as lost and confused about her personal life now as she had at twenty-one.

She had no idea what she was going to do. She hated this feeling and she knew there was no list she could make or plans she could set in motion that would allay this fear. It stemmed from so deep inside of her that she knew it was time to just face it. Sometimes owning a fear would make it into something she could conquer. She'd done it one other time. When she'd turned thirty and realized that she was going to be on her own after she'd broken up with her boyfriend at the time, Wendall.

"This is the same thing," she muttered to herself. "Just say it out loud. Own it."

Own it.

"I'm not lovable. I have too many edges and rules that I surround myself with. No man can fit into the mold I've created. And Slade isn't going to wake up and realize he loves me."

Her voice cracked a little on the last note. "But I still love him."

There.

She'd said it.

She owned it.

"I love him, but he doesn't love me. Okay. But I can't stop loving him."

Oh, man, she was losing it. But there it was. That was the truth. Regardless of what happened with their engagement, she was probably going to love Slade for the rest of her life. And she had to find a way to live with that. A way to explain that to their child.

The child she wasn't even sure that Slade would be a father to. And that hurt her. That he wouldn't want to share a life with her and their baby. But that had nothing to do with her. And she had to figure out how to forge a life without him. Unless she could find out what his fear was…

Was it possible that she'd be able to help him see the other side? See that together they would be better?

Eleven

Back at her condo after the spa that afternoon, Melinda took Pixie out on the balcony and stood at the railing looking down at the city. Up here, it seemed so much easier to make decisions than it did when she was sitting next to her sister or when she was with Slade. The truth was that Angela had been right. If she was in love with Slade, she would figure out a way to make him be a part of her life now and forever.

The thing was she didn't want to manipulate him into loving her and committing to her. She didn't want to pressure him into staying in a relationship that would feel like a trap to him.

He'd shared the story of his parents' marriage and she'd seen firsthand her own parents' happy marriage break down. She certainly didn't want to end up like that. She knew from her own experience that having two parents who felt trapped wasn't necessarily better than just having one. Or she thought it wouldn't be. She had no idea what it would be like to grow up having only one parent. She'd lost her mom ten years ago and that had been hard enough. What would her child face if only she raised it?

Pixie barked and ran back into the condo, and Melinda followed her. She'd given Slade a key, but he had yet to use it without texting her first to let her know he was coming over. They had debated moving in together because they both knew that some of the more mean-spirited social bloggers had commented on the fact that the only time they were together was to hook up.

But Melinda had never let anyone push her into doing anything in her life and wasn't about to start now. Which was another argument for not doing the things that would make Slade feel like he had to stay engaged to her, that he had to marry her.

She wouldn't be able to handle the guilt that went along with that. The fact was she wanted this to sort itself out. But she'd never been able to leave things be. Her father liked to say that everything happened in its own time, but she had always been too impatient to wait.

She wanted things to happen in Melinda's time. When she wanted it, not when it was right.

"Hello," she heard Slade call out. "Where's your mistress, Pix?"

"I'm here. Just enjoying the sun and the peace up here," she called back. "I have some sweet tea out here if you're thirsty. There's also beer in the fridge."

"Sweet tea sounds perfect," he said as he came onto the balcony. He pulled her into his arms and leaned in to kiss her, but his mouth skimmed along her cheek. It felt different now that she'd acknowledged that she loved him. She still got that rush that she always did when she saw him but she knew that once the media stopped bothering her, he'd leave. And that hurt. This was exactly what she'd been trying to avoid.

"I noticed that one of the bloggers that has been watching you has a drone so we might not be alone."

She literally started shaking with outrage. Why did anyone believe they had the right to spy on her? She could understand their curiosity about her relationship...but a drone? That was too much. "They're going too far."

"I agree," he said, stepping back and rubbing his hands up and down her bare arms. "But I wanted you to know."

"I'm going to call the building managers. Surely there's some sort of legal reason why they can't fly it over the condos," Melinda said.

"I think we need to give the media something to

print. Let's face it, we've been pretty low-key for the last week or so," he said.

She nodded. Giving them something to talk about was the entire reason they had gotten engaged. Her doubts had made her reluctant to walk around, letting anyone see the two of them together. She knew it was going to be much harder—much more humiliating—when they ended things if there were all those pictures of them being all lovey-dovey.

The knot in the pit of her stomach intensified and she honestly felt like she might throw up. She thought she could control it and then realized she couldn't. She tried to walk all ladylike into her living room and then as soon as she was inside bolted for the bathroom. She heard Slade behind her. The heels on his dress shoes echoed behind her on the marble floor and she knew he was saying something, but she was so focused on not throwing up until she was in the bathroom she couldn't comprehend or respond.

She got into the bathroom just in time. She heard Slade behind her as she finished throwing up. He handed her a towel to wipe her mouth and then a cup of water to rinse with. Then he pulled her into his arms and held her to him. Just a hug that offered comfort and she started crying. There was no reason for the tears, except she wasn't holding things together the way she usually could.

This entire situation was insane. Not what she had planned for herself or her unborn child or Slade.

She always had a plan and things usually worked out the way she planned them, but this time they weren't. She had no idea how to get back on track and it seemed the more she tried, the harder it was.

He held the back of her head, lightly massaging her scalp, and she just closed her eyes and pretended she hadn't just gotten sick or cried in his arms. Finally, she felt slightly better and stepped back.

"I'm sorry about that."

"Don't be. You're pregnant and life is a bit stressful right now. Do you feel up to a walk around downtown? Just something for the paparazzi to snap some pictures of and then we can come home, and I'll make dinner for you."

"You can cook?" she asked.

"Yes, and I'm pretty damned good at it. What do you say?"

She nodded. "That sounds good to me. I'll go get changed. I guess you'll need to change as well."

"I will. I'm glad I had some of my clothes sent over here."

"Me too," she said, thinking of his clothes in the master bedroom closet and in a drawer she'd emptied for him. Though last night she'd realized that wasn't helping her keep their lives separate.

A romantic walk… Not his smartest idea given that he should be trying to put some distance between him and Melinda. But here he was. Pixie didn't seem that happy about it either. She was on a leash and her little jeweled collar sparkled in the sunlight. Everyone who walked past them smiled at the cute dachshund and when they glanced up and saw him and Melinda holding hands and looking to the world like lovers who had the world on a string, they smiled at them as well.

Only, he felt the way that Melinda's hand tightened in his each time that happened. He knew this kind of outward deception wasn't her thing. He didn't need to be a mind reader to know that the further they got into the engagement, the harder it was going to be for her to pull off a breakup.

If he were a different man, he'd make the temporary promise he had made her into a real one. And he wasn't going to lie to himself, he'd thought about it more than once. But then he'd see one of his uncles at a distance or another news alert about the Bartelli family and he knew that he had to stay resolute.

He wasn't about to put any child of Melinda's through what he had gone through as a child. He had clawed his way out of the Bartelli family, but it would be impossible to protect a child of his from them. He knew from his own behavior as a teenager that rebellion was a big part of why he had to keep his distance from the child.

It would have probably been better if he had never gone out with her. But he couldn't undo the past and he had always used his mistakes to get stronger.

They stopped at a nearby café, needing a drink from the heat. After they were seated in a dog-friendly section, Pixie drank water from a collapsible bowl that Melinda had pulled from her bag and then she curled up on the scarf that Melinda laid down for her.

"What are you thinking about?" she asked, after the waitress took their drink orders. "You looked so fierce I think the waitress was afraid to ask what you wanted to drink."

He tried to smile but that was gone. They were in the relative privacy of the café and he didn't have to keep up the sappy so-in-love vibe he'd had going on the street. "Nothing."

"I can tell it was something," she said.

He just shrugged. He wasn't obliged to share everything with Melinda.

"Listen, if you want me to keep doing this, then you need to be honest with me. We can't be lying in public and in private... Well, maybe you can, but I can't. I won't. So either you level with me or I'm out of here."

He had seen her worked up before and, no lie, it did turn him on to see her passionate but not like this. She was angry and hurt and he was to blame. How many times did he need to see proof that he was the completely wrong man for her?

"You're Slade Bartelli," a tall man in a Stetson

and a serious expression said as he came over to their table. Pixie got up and danced over toward the man, who bent down and petted her. Not so fierce when he smiled at the little dog.

Melinda glanced up at the man, who looked like he didn't like Slade very much. Slade stood up and held out his hand.

"I am. This is Melinda Perry," he said. "And you are?"

"Nathan Battle, the sheriff of Royal, Texas." He turned to Melinda. "Ma'am. Are you related to Sterling Perry?"

"He's my father," she said.

He tipped his hat toward her and continued to stand, as did Slade, and the sheriff turned his attention back toward Slade.

"Your father's activities are starting to encroach on several of the more prominent citizens of Royal and I don't like that much," Nathan said.

"I'm sorry to hear that, sir," Slade said. "I have nothing to do with my father's business. In fact, I'm the CEO of Conti Enterprises. I'd offer to have a word with him, but he doesn't listen to anyone."

"Would you sit down, Sheriff?" Melinda asked.

"I can't, ma'am. I'm in town on business and thought I'd kill two birds with one stone."

"What is the other business that brings you to Houston?" Melinda asked, afraid that it might have something to do with the grisly murder of the man found on her father's construction site at the new Texas Cattleman's Club.

"I'm investigating the Vincent Hamm murder. So far I haven't been able to get much information from Detective Zoe Warren, who is in charge of the Houston investigation, so I've come to do some of my own digging."

"Isn't it a Houston case?" Melinda asked, wondering why the Royal sheriff was investigating. Was there more to the case than just murder? Did it somehow tie to Royal?

"It is, but Hamm was from Royal and a family friend. I've promised his father I'd find out what happened. You know a text was sent from Vincent's Perry Holdings phone—after he was dead."

"Who would do such a thing?" Melinda asked. "That's horrible."

"It's awful," Slade added. "Some people will do anything to cover their tracks."

"Yes, they will," the sheriff said. "Well, I'll leave you two to your drinks. If you think of anything that could help with my investigation, give me a call."

He handed them his card and then walked away. Slade watched him leave before finally sitting back down. He looked at the card for a moment before tucking it into the inside pocket of his jacket.

Slade Bartelli hadn't been exactly what Nathan had been expecting. He had a firm handshake and he'd been respectful and forthright with him. Nathan rubbed the back of his neck as he headed to the Houston Police Department. He was frustrated by the lack of suspects in Vincent Hamm's murder.

He knew he'd stopped and warned Bartelli because of that. He normally wasn't the kind of sheriff who threatened men like Slade—a billionaire entrepreneur and not a street thug. He waited for Detective Zoe Warren and decided he was ready to be back in Royal.

He liked being on his own turf. He missed his wife, Amanda, and the diner she ran back in Royal and the coffee that she always had waiting for him when he stopped by. He didn't relish going back to Royal without some answers for Vincent's family. They were all beside themselves, and he admitted to himself that that was one thing he really hated about his job. Talking to the victims' families. Especially when he knew them as well as he did the Hamms.

"Sheriff Battle, what can I do for you?" Zoe asked as she met him in the waiting area.

"Just following up to see where you stand on the Hamm investigation," he said.

"Come back to my desk and I'll update you," she said. "I have to be honest. We don't have much to go on."

He followed her through the precinct to her desk and he realized he started to relax being in the familiar environment. He liked cops and he felt most at home when he was surrounded by them.

"As you know, I've had Sterling Perry in for questioning. The man was cagey and not very cooperative. Could be because he's been under investigation since the first time I talked to him." She shrugged. "But he didn't add anything new. Neither did Liam Morrow, who, along with the construction crew, found the body. And none of Hamm's colleagues have anything to add either."

"Hmm, I don't like that. Someone has to know something," Nathan said.

"I agree. I'm shaking some trees… I was hoping that since you were here, maybe you'd heard something in Royal?" she said with a question in her voice.

"Nothing yet. But I'll keep poking around and let you know what I find," he said.

"Good. I'll keep you in the loop if I get any breaks on this case," she said. "I know this one is personal for you. That always makes me more determined to solve it."

"I doubt you are ever not determined," he said, standing up.

"Very true," she admitted with a smile.

He shook her hand before leaving the station. When he got out on the street, he took a moment to think about the suspects. Hell, there weren't any. But Sterling Perry being cagey… That bothered him. He would put out a few feelers and see what else he could find out about Perry and his business.

Melinda watched Slade as he sat back down. He was on edge and looked like he wanted to punch someone. It was the first time she'd seen him like this. She could tell he didn't like being treated like a criminal when he wasn't one.

She didn't like it either. Slade was a good man. The man she loved. How dare that sheriff stop and talk to him like that.

"I cannot tell you how many times I've had that conversation with law enforcement," he said.

"I can't believe it," she said, realizing that there was a lot more to Slade's life than she had glimpsed. "I mean, your dad of course has a reputation, but you've never done anything outside the law. Is this what you are afraid of if we got married?"

He looked at her, his dark gaze a cocktail of emotions that she had a hard time reading. Anger and remorse and something else she couldn't identify.

"Hell, Mels, of course, I don't want you subject to anything like that. I hate that he felt justified in coming up to talk to me when I was with you. I'm not a criminal. I have lived my life above reproach... but this kind of thing isn't going to just disappear."

"It isn't," she said, her heart aching at the thought of Slade spending the rest of his life alone and isolated from her and their child to protect them. It was an honorable sentiment, but he shouldn't be alone. He didn't have to be. "I can handle that, Slade. I'm not as frail as you might think I am."

"I know that, woman. That doesn't mean I want you to have to fight the battle that comes with my last name," he said.

"You're not asking me to, I'm asking you to let me," she said. "Do you understand? For me, this is something that I can't just ignore. I care deeply about you. I can't stand the thought that anyone feels as if they can question you about your father's crimes."

He nodded, leaned over and kissed her so softly and sweetly that the love she was trying desperately not to confess almost spilled out.

"I'm sorry you had to see it," he said, as he lifted his head. "I have to remember that neither of us is responsible for our family's actions."

"That's okay," she said. "You're not your father."

"No, I'm not," he said. "Neither are you."

She sat back from him and narrowed her eyes, not sure why he would bring up her father. "What are you saying?"

"Just that you must endure some questions about your father. That's pretty tough to ignore."

"Not for me," she said. "The rumors aren't true. You must know that."

He shrugged. "I'm used to dealing with people whispering behind my back. You might have to get used to that on your own, even without adding the Bartelli name to the mix."

"What are you saying?"

"That people think your father had something to do with Vincent Hamm's murder," he said.

"If that were true, I think Sheriff Battle would have brought it up," she said, wondering where he was leading with all of this. "But he didn't. Don't try to paint my father with the same brush as yours."

"I'm not painting him with anything. I'm simply saying your father has rumors swirling all around him."

She shook her head, trying not to let her anger get the better of her, but the more he talked, the worse he was making it. "We were talking about you, Slade. Not my dad. Who, by the way, is nothing like your father."

"Well, that has yet to be seen," Slade said.

"Why would you say such a thing?" she asked, angry and hurt that he'd even think her father would be part of anything illegal, especially murder. She stood up and grabbed her purse and Pixie's leash, glaring down at him.

"How dare you, Slade Bartelli."

He stopped her by grabbing her arm gently. Her handbag hit him in the arm but he ignored it. He couldn't let her walk away like this. Not now. He pulled her into his arms when he noticed some of the other patrons looking at them, and kissed her gently, but she turned her head. She was ticked at him and fair enough.

"People are watching," he said, under his breath.

She looked at him with such disdain that he knew his solution was going to kill whatever had been simmering between them. She was something he was afraid to keep for himself, and he was doing what he always did when he had someone in his life who cared. Driving them away.

"Let's finish our drinks so we can both leave together," he said.

"Let's go. I can't do this right now," she said.

"All right, let's go," he said loudly, linking their hands together and leading her and Pixie out to the street. Wanting to get inside and find privacy, he decided not to walk back to her condo. Instead, he hailed a taxi.

He wrapped his arm around her shoulder and held her close to his body and he was pretty sure he was the only one who knew that she pinched him on his side when he did it, but she smiled up at him at the same time.

He simply smiled back and as soon as they were at her building, he got out and held the door for her as she scooped up Pixie. He put his hand on the small of her back as he guided her toward her building. A flurry of paparazzi was waiting at the entrance, snapping pictures and yelling questions.

This was crazy. How had he ever thought his plan was going to help? But he'd had no other idea how to protect her and he hadn't been ready to stay goodbye. He still wasn't. But was he holding on for himself only?

He knew that this was harder for Melinda than she'd ever admit. A clean break would have been better. He should have said he didn't want to be a father and just walked away. Better to let her think he was an ass than to break her heart.

As soon as they were across the lobby and in the private elevator bank, she stepped away from him.

"You don't have to come up."

"I do. We're not done with this," he said. Granted, his father had a much longer history of criminal activity than any Perry did. But her father had been making some interesting choices of late, so Slade's comment wasn't completely out of line. She had to know what people were saying. In fact, she probably did but she didn't want to hear it from him.

"I'm done. I can't believe you accused my father of murder. I've defended you more times than I care to admit, and everyone knows your family is organized crime. And I've taken your word that you're not involved," she said, jamming the call button for the elevator with more force than was necessary.

"Yes, you have. With good reason," he added. "When have I lied to you?" It bothered him that everyone judged him to be like his father without knowing him, but he couldn't say something… Hell, he knew he'd lashed out because that damned sheriff had made him remember he wasn't good enough for Melinda. It wasn't like that would be the last time in his life when a law enforcement official would question him, even though he had never done a single damned thing that was against the law. "Even when lying would have benefited me, I've always been honest with you."

She sighed. "I know. I know, Slade. God, I'm sorry, it's just that your question hit a little too close to home. And I'm tired of pretending. I…" She hesitated, as if she didn't want to finish her thought, then finally said, "I like you, and I don't want to break up with you because you're afraid of commitment."

"I wish it were just that. But it's more. My family isn't like yours. Mine is really involved in things that are illegal and it took a lot of struggling for me to break free from them. I know if I claim you and the child as my own, my father isn't going to stay out of the child's life. We have to do it the way I described, or you're going—"

"Are you saying if it weren't for your father, you'd stay with me?" she asked.

He hesitated.

"No, you're not saying that. Is that the excuse you tell yourself to make it sound better?" she questioned. The elevator car arrived, and she set Pixie down, letting the dog walk on before her.

"It's not an excuse," he said, but as soon as he said it, he knew that it was. He didn't want to chance loving her. He'd seen what had happened with his parents' marriage. He knew that two people from such diverse backgrounds would have to struggle to make a situation like this one work.

He could handle her pissed off and mad at him, but hurt, broken—the way his mom had been after her divorce or the way his long-ago fiancée had been after they'd split up—no. He couldn't handle that. He needed to know that she was okay.

"You're right, Mels. But the truth is I can't handle being the man who disappoints you."

"You already are," she said.

"Not like I will," he admitted.

"Oh, Slade," she said, taking his hand.

And that was the moment when he should have walked away, but he let her lead him onto the elevator because he needed her more than he wanted to protect her.

Twelve

The next morning when she woke up, she found Slade sitting on the edge of the bed, head bowed as he looked down at his feet. His muscled back was strained and she saw the stress in him.

"Slade? Honey, what's the matter?" she asked.

He glanced over at her and smiled. "Morning, baby cakes. Nothing. Just a text from my dad."

"What does he want?"

"To see me," Slade said. "He sends me a text once a week, asking to see me."

"Why?"

"Because I haven't seen him or knowingly been in his company since I turned eighteen."

"Why not?"

"It's complicated," Slade said.

"I'm your pretend fiancée who is pregnant with your baby that no one knows about, so I think I can handle complicated," she said.

He gave a laugh. "Yeah, I guess you can."

He turned and piled some pillows against the headboard and shifted around until he was lying against them. "I took Pixie out by the way."

"Thank you. Now you were saying about your father…" Somehow, she knew she had to get to the bottom of whatever it was that made him not want to be a family man. From her experience with her own family and from watching some of her friends marry and divorce, she knew that relationships were often influenced by the couple's own parents.

"You're not going to let this go, are you?" he asked.

She shook her head. "Nope. I have a vested interest in this, honey. Someday, our baby is going to ask me about his paternal grandfather, and I want to be able to answer honestly."

"This isn't going to make it easier," he said.

"Just tell me," she said, pulling the sheet up under her armpits and smiling over at him.

"Okay…so after my mom died, I lived with my grandparents and they had custody of me. It had been decided that it would be better for everyone if they continued raising me. It was a good life, but I was curious about my father. My memories of him had been tied to my childhood and my nonno hated my dad so I didn't know if that had colored my opinion of him," Slade said, not looking at her but looking at his own feet as he kept crossing and uncrossing his legs on the bed.

It was odd to her because Slade wasn't normally a nervous, fidgety person, but this story wasn't something easy for him to tell and it was over twenty years old.

"That makes sense. No matter how my parents fought, I am very glad that I got to know them both and that they were together for us," Melinda said. And she was. She wanted that for her child. She knew in her heart that she and Slade were very different people, but she also firmly believed that children needed to know both of their parents to be successful in life.

"Are you?" he asked gently, but the more she pushed him on this, the more defensive he felt. "I think that might be because you had them both. But if your father was like mine, you might not feel the same way."

"What are you trying to say?" she asked. "You know you're not anything like your own father."

"Am I?" he asked.

"Unless you've been lying to me and deceiving me since we started dating. Have you?"

He cursed and stood up, walking away from the bed and over to the glass doors that overlooked her balcony and then the city. She wondered what he saw. What was he trying not to tell her?

She got out of bed and put on her floral-print robe, belting it at the waist. Pixie trotted over to her and Melinda bent down to pet her and gave her a cuddle before walking over to where Slade stood. She put her hand on his back and leaned around, looking up at his face.

She remembered when they'd made love in her condo at the glass door. So much of her life was tied to his now. She knew she'd have a hard time separating from him when he walked away. But she also had no regrets. She might be confused about single parenthood and how her life was going to shake out, but she was also excited about entering this new phase of her life.

One she would never have had if not for Slade.

"Okay, so you're a teenager and rebellious and… you go see your dad?"

"Yeah," he said, putting his arm around her shoulder and hugging her to him. She wrapped her arm around his waist and put her other hand on his chest.

This confession haunted him probably the same way that the time she'd run away when she'd been in fifth grade had dogged her for a long time. She'd gone to keep her friend from being alone, but the repercussions had been a deterioration in her relationship with her mom, who thought she'd left because of the fighting at home.

"It's okay. Whatever you did," she said.

"It's not," he said. "I started sneaking out to see him and he's a really funny guy, smart and charming. I couldn't for the life of me figure out why my grandparents hated him or even why my mom left him. After about six weeks, he asked me if I wanted to go to work with him. See what my Bartelli family was like."

She had a sinking feeling in the pit of her stomach. She should stop him from telling her anything more, but at the same time she wanted to know exactly what had happened. She needed to see the entire picture, so she knew what she was fighting.

"I bet you were curious. You'd never met them, had you?"

"Not since Mom and I had left," he said. "I went with him and met my uncles and the rest of my goombahs."

"What's a *goombah*?" she asked.

"Well, in the Conti family, it means friends who are close like family. But for the Bartellis... Well, it's more like anyone associated with their crime family. This thing I'm about to tell you, Melinda... I've never told anyone."

She nodded. "Your secret is safe with me."

And it was. She loved this man and would do whatever she had to protect him.

"Some of my uncles were like my dad. Funny, charming. But some of the others wanted me to prove myself. They thought I had no place in the Bartelli family. And my goombahs were even more adamant. So, Dad pulled me aside and said if I went on a job, proved myself, they'd leave me be and that would be the end of it."

"What kind of job?" she asked.

"I had no idea. I had been to work with Nonno and though I knew the rumors about the mob stuff, I still didn't really get what that meant. I mean, I had a vague idea from watching *The Godfather* and *Goodfellas* as a point of reference but that wasn't Houston. Wasn't my Italian American family, you know? God, saying this out loud makes me realize how naive I was."

She hugged him. "You don't have to say anything else."

"Are you sure?" he asked.

"Yes. You're nothing like your father," she said. "You don't have to tell me about him and how it affected you for me to see that."

She watched his face and noticed the ways his eyes flickered away from her, as if he didn't want her to see the truth.

"Right?" she asked him.

He took a deep breath. "The truth is I liked being part of his crew. And though the…"

She didn't want to know if he'd killed someone

or beat someone up… Did she? "Activity?" she supplied.

"Yes. Though the activity wasn't something I could stomach, I liked being part of the family. Having the other guys around me. It was hard to walk away from. Harder than I'd like to admit. And then because I had ridden with him for a few weeks, my uncles and cousins didn't want me to walk away."

"What did you do? Did you kill someone?"

"No. I'd never do that. In fact, that was why I left. Like I said, riding with the crew was fun. It was like having brothers and for the first time in my life, I wasn't getting the stink eye from others because I was a Bartelli. I was accepted just for who I was. My dad sent me on collection runs to pick up money and stuff like that. But on my last ride…things went south, and my cousin Pauley pulled his gun and shot two guys. I just stood there. I have to be honest, Melinda. I was freaking out. This guy had been laughing and joking with me seconds before.

"Pauley took one look at my face and knew that I wasn't going to be able to help him and told me to get out of there. I did. Ran straight back to my grandparents and I haven't spoken to my dad since."

He saw the horror on her face, and he didn't blame her at all. Eighteen had been a long time ago and he'd been young and stupid. But the worst part was believing he could walk away. That the weeks he'd spent running with the Bartelli family wouldn't have a lasting effect. Until he got engaged. Then he saw the truth. How some of his goombahs had never forgiven him for the way he left. And they never would.

"That's why I can't be the family man you want me to be," he said, quietly.

She shook her head. "I'm horrified that you had to go through that. That your father put you in that situation. I knew you wouldn't knowingly harm anyone."

He could hear her working her way through the story he'd just told her, and this was the thing about Melinda that always made him regret that he wasn't a better man. She was going to find a way to use that to make him stronger in her own eyes. He'd honestly never met anyone who was determined to see the best in people. But he knew he wasn't the best. He'd taken the easy way out too many times. Running back to Nonno where he'd known that his father wouldn't follow.

His grandparents had been disappointed, but they'd understood his need to see for himself the man his father was. His dad tried to talk to him, but Slade had refused. He didn't want any part of that life. His cousins had beat him up after school and threatened to kill him if he ratted out Pauley, which Slade had no intention of doing. He wanted nothing to do with the Bartelli family. But once he left to go to college in Austin, he called the tip line and reported the crime. He hadn't been able to live with the knowledge that he'd witnessed those deaths. It didn't matter that the men who'd been killed had been rough criminals.

"I could never hurt anyone," he agreed. "But that's what the Bartelli family does. And if I'm in our child's life, then you and our child will be targeted by the family. I have no way of protecting you." He'd just named his deepest, darkest fear out loud and to be honest, it sounded even worse now that he'd done that. He wanted to be the man who protected her, not the one who led her to a place she could never come back from.

"You have one," she said.

"What's that?" he asked. Melinda was smart; maybe she saw something he didn't.

"Go to your dad, tell him you want a new life with me and that he needs to ensure that his family knows you aren't going to ever be a part of it," she said.

"My dad... Why would he do that? He wouldn't lift a finger to help my fiancée."

"Did you ask him to?" she asked carefully.

"I sent word to him through one of my cousins," he said. He hadn't been able to ask his father; he'd been afraid he might say no. That had been the one thing that Slade had never been able to understand about himself. He wanted to hate his father but he'd never been able to. He still loved his dad.

Still wanted him to be the kind of father who protected his kid… Damn, his own kid was going to feel the same way.

He didn't know how he was going to live with knowing he was hurting Melinda's child.

"I can only tell you that from what I've observed, some men mellow as they get older," she said, "and if he has a chance to see our child…maybe that will be enough."

He shook his head. "He's dead to me. I won't ask him for anything."

"You're being stubborn about this."

He was, but there were some things that he wouldn't back down on, and his father was one of them. He didn't know if it was pride or just resentment that his dad had failed him so massively when he'd been a teenager, but he wasn't going to ask him for anything. Not now. Not even for Melinda.

"Maybe, but this isn't something I'm willing to do," he said. "I don't expect you to understand. Despite his shady dealings, your father has always been a solid figure in your life."

She chewed her lower lip and put one hand on her hip. "I think you're being an ass about this. We could have everything. A real engagement and a real wedding. We could raise this baby together. I would do anything that I needed to in order to make that happen."

He knew she would. She'd been like that from the

moment she found out about the baby. Or from the moment he'd found out. She'd looked at him with hope in her eyes and he'd panicked and done what he could to protect her. But he was being the man Melinda needed him to be and not himself.

Every time he'd stepped away from owning his actions, it had backfired. Much like this entire morning was. She wanted something from him because she thought if he did this—went to his dad and asked him for something—then everything was going to be fine.

But it wouldn't be. He was a man who'd spent all of his adult life on his own, not having anyone dependent on him, and that enabled him to make risky decisions in business. To have fun when he wanted to. And not hurt anyone else because of his family name.

"I wish it were that easy, Melinda. That you could wave your magic wand and I'd become the man you want me to be. I think you've been seeing me as someone else. Some kind of prince like those heroes in the books you like to read. But I'm not that guy."

She shook her head.

"You could be."

He didn't think it was possible to hurt like this, but he did. He was frozen with a desire to be that man she wanted at the same time he was facing the reality of who he was. He didn't want to disappoint her but if he weren't true to himself, what kind of man would he be?

He wasn't willing to risk it or try to find out.

"I'm not going to do it," he said. "I will not talk to my father. I can't be a family man, because it's not the life I chose. And we're not children, Melinda, so I know you can understand that."

She wasn't having it and he didn't blame her. But he had never felt anything like this fear he felt when he thought of her getting to know his Bartelli family. He knew how quickly they could turn from normal to criminal. In a blink of an eye. He didn't want her or any child of theirs near that kind of life. And if that meant he had to spend the rest of his life without her...then so be it.

He'd rather she be alive and safe than with him for a short time.

"You could if I meant more to you," she said.

"You know what you mean to me," he retorted. He was trying to be cool, but it was harder than he thought. He was putting her first. Why couldn't she see that and accept it and just let this lie?

"Do I?"

"Yes, you do and I'm not going to play this kind of game. One of the things I've always admired about you is how forthright you are. I've never had to pretend to be someone I'm not with you."

"Good thing," she said. "We know how much you have to be you."

She turned away and he realized that he needed to do something to salvage this. "I'm sorry."

She glanced back over at him, hope in her eyes, and he knew that unless he made a clean break, she was always going to be hoping he'd be that better man.

"Me too. I love you, Slade. I haven't wanted to say it until we sorted everything else out, but my feelings aren't going to change. I want you by my side when the child is born. I want to have a family with you. I can't keep lying about that. I think when I said yes to the charade, I figured you'd come around to making it real. Have you?"

Everything inside of him froze. She loved him. He had both wanted that and feared it from the moment he'd seen those pregnancy tests lined up on her bathroom counter. Melinda Perry was everything he never knew he wanted in a woman and nothing hurt him more than knowing if he tied his life to hers, she'd be bound by the same prejudice and gossip and rumors that had plagued him his entire life. And she deserved better.

This was his nightmare. She was asking him for something that he'd already promised himself he'd never take a chance on. "Melinda, didn't you hear what I said?"

"I did, but I thought if you knew how much I care about you…if you saw me taking a chance on us, then you'd be able to as well," she said. "Can you?"

Dammit.

He couldn't think of anything to say. He just stood there, watching her, and he saw her hope die and finally she shook her head.

"I deserve a man who can stand by my side, and our child deserves a father who will be a part of its life. I understand your fears, but you were a boy, alone and unsure. Our child could have both of us. If not, it will have me, and I will never let anyone—including you—hurt him or her."

"I understand. I can't be that man."

"If you can't be the man I need you to be, then I guess this is it," she said.

He watched as she took his ring from her finger—the ring Nonna had given him to give to her—and she handed it to him. "I'm going to get in the shower and when I get out, I expect you to be gone."

She walked away from him and all he could do was watch her leave. He gathered his stuff and walked away.

Thirteen

Melinda hadn't been surprised when she came out of the bathroom and Slade was gone. What did surprise her was that he'd taken all of his stuff from her condo. It was as if he'd never been there except for the lingering scent of his deodorant, which he must have put on before leaving. Pixie was sitting on her pillow in the middle of a sunspot near the glass door, but Melinda couldn't get her normal joy from seeing her dachshund.

Instead, she sat at her vanity and avoided looking herself in the eyes. She felt like crying but was trying not to because she had meetings to get through and without a doubt, the paparazzi would still be dogging her all day. She leaned forward, putting her head in her hands. She felt a little sick to her stomach and wasn't sure if it was because she'd taken a gamble on love and lost or if it was the pregnancy.

She'd told herself and Slade she'd rather go it alone than with a man who didn't want to be with her, but she didn't want that. Sure, she could do it by herself but who wanted to do this alone. The nausea passed and she lifted her head. She wasn't about to be someone that others felt sorry for. So that meant getting dressed and acting like she was happy with the choices she'd made this morning.

But she wasn't.

After last night, she'd believed that Slade really cared about her, that he'd never let anyone hurt them. But now she knew he was afraid to be hurt. It was as if he thought that she would walk away when things got tough, like that fiancée who had left him.

But she had steel in her backbone. He should have known that by now.

"Play some music, Jeeves," she said to her in-home assistant.

The first song that came on was "Let's Stay Together" by Al Green. That oldie that she and Slade had danced to on their first date. He'd taken her to Galveston for a private dinner on the beach and then they'd danced under the stars.

Tears burned the back of her eyes.

"Skip this song, Jeeves, and play 'Shout Out to My Ex' by Little Mix instead."

The song switched and she forced herself to get up from the vanity stool and sing along with the song until she didn't feel like crying anymore. The music continued with more dance and party tunes as she finished getting ready for her day.

She went to work and sat in meetings and smiled at everyone she saw throughout the day and if she were honest, she thought she did a pretty good job of acting like everything was normal. Until Angela texted to invite her out to dinner at the Flying Saucer. She accepted, then realized that fooling her twin that she wasn't heartbroken was going to be a lot harder than fooling everyone else. She went home and changed into a pair of jeans that felt too constricting around the middle, even though her belly hadn't changed. So she switched for a long flowy dress and a cardigan because the air-conditioning was sometimes too cold for her and went to meet her twin.

Angela was already waiting for her when she got there and waved from her table toward the back of the restaurant. She heard the music from the bar as she moved past the tables and noticed a family sitting to her right. Unbidden, an image of herself and a child sitting together popped into her head. She smiled and realized that she was going to be fine without Slade. She'd miss him and there would be times when she'd feel his absence, but she knew she'd figure out a way to make being a single mom work for her.

Angela got up and hugged her and then slid back into the booth. "I didn't know what to order you to drink. I mean with the, uh, you know."

"I know. Sweet tea will be fine," Melinda said when the waitress came over. They both placed their order. Because they'd eaten here so often, they knew the menu by heart.

As soon as they were alone, Angela leaned forward. "How are you doing? Did you get Slade to commit?"

She shook her head. "I'm doing okay. No, I didn't get him to commit and I gave him an ultimatum… You know, we might need to consider the reason I'm single is that I'm sort of an all-or-nothing kind of girl."

Angela squeezed her hand. "Nothing wrong with that. Is there anything I can do?"

"You've already done it," she said, looking around. Being alone, she knew, was going to be difficult until she could think about Slade and not feel like crying. She was grateful her sister had asked her to dinner. "I really needed this tonight. I've been fake smiling my way through the day and with you, I can just be me."

"You know it, girl," Angela said. "Want me to kick his ass for you?"

She smiled at her sister. "I love you, you know that, right?"

Her twin nodded. "Do I need to go and find Slade Bartelli?"

"No. But thank you for that. I'm pretty sure this was rough on him as well."

"Okay, then. He always struck me as smarter than that. Do you want to talk about it?" Angela asked.

They both sat back as the waitress delivered two French dip sandwiches and a hot pretzel on the side. Melinda broke off a piece of the pretzel before answering her sister.

"Not now," she said. "It's too fresh right now."

"Okay. Then if you don't mind, I could actually use your help," Angela said while they enjoyed their dinner.

She hoped her sister wouldn't ask her to help plan her and Ryder's wedding. But she would say yes if Angela did. "What with?"

"Do you know a Willem Inwood? The name sounds so familiar and I wondered if he was a family friend or maybe someone we went to school with?" Angela asked.

Relief flooded through her. Something that had nothing to do with weddings. Thank the stars. No one came to mind, so she shook her head. "The name sounds sort of familiar, but I can't place it. I'll look through my address book at home."

"Address book?"

"Yes. I mean, I digitized everything but kept all my old paper books. One of them has Mom's handwriting in it and I couldn't part with that," Melinda said.

"Of course not, and it makes total sense that you'd have your hard copies. Don't want to take a chance on losing anything important, right?"

"Exactly."

They chatted and Melinda even laughed a bit with her sister before going home and it was only when she was back in her bedroom, after putting Pixie out and getting ready for bed, that she realized she was lying to herself about being okay with the breakup. She missed Slade and could only hope that in time the pain would lessen.

Angela called Ryder to see if he'd be coming over later, but he sounded frustrated with his Currin Oil employee relations investigation and she just gave him her best and hung up. She wished there were something she could do to help him fix this problem. Some way to figure out where Willem Inwood was. That would give Ryder a chance to actually get some decent answers.

Seeing her sister tonight and the way she was heartbroken over Slade, Angela knew she didn't want to let that happen to her and Ryder. She knew that Melinda was strong and that little baby she was carrying was going to be the most spoiled child on the planet if Angela had anything to say about it. But for right now, her sister was going to have to go it alone and figure out what kind of life she was going to make for herself and the baby.

She tossed her keys on her hall table and poured herself a glass of wine before going to sit on the couch.

Willem Inwood.

She wanted to help find this man so that she could maybe prove her father had nothing to do with the problems Ryder was going through. She wanted both men to get along and not be at each other's throats all the time. It would be hard to be happily married if her father and husband were always trying to implicate each other in crimes.

But she couldn't place the name Willem Inwood. Maybe Tatiana would know the man. She looked at the clock and seeing it was only a bit past ten o'clock, knew her best friend would still be awake. She and Tatiana Havery had usually hung out more often than they had in the last few weeks due to their busy schedules. It was time for a catch-up.

She would have invited Tatiana to dinner tonight but she knew her sister might want some one-on-one time.

She hit the button to call Tatiana.

"Hey, girl," Tatiana said. "How's things in lovey-dovey central?"

"Hey. They're good," she said, afraid to let on that she was feeling more and more out of control with Ryder while he was dealing with the business mess. That things were good, they were still committed but he was keeping her at arm's length.

"Glad to hear it. So, what are you two up to tonight?"

"Oh, Ryder's working. I just had dinner with Mels and now I'm back home," she said. She injected a note of happiness into her voice.

"How's your sister? I've seen way more of her on the society page and on the internet than Melinda usually likes," Tatiana said.

"Oh, she's struggling but she's managing it," she said, knowing that Melinda wouldn't want Tatiana to know everything that was going on with Slade.

"Not surprised. You Perrys always do," Tatiana said.

"Actually, I was calling because of Ryder's work," Angela said, taking a sip of her wine as she curled her legs underneath her.

"I don't know much about oil refineries."

"Ha. Me either. The thing is that Ryder is having some employee issues and he mentioned one of his managers—Willem Inwood. That name sounds so familiar, but I can't place it. Do you know him?"

"No. I don't know him. The name's not ringing any bells," Tatiana said. "How are the wedding plans coming?"

Angela sighed. Maybe she was just imagining she'd heard of Inwood because she wanted a quick resolution to Ryder's problems and to prove her dad had nothing to do with it. "We haven't had much of a chance to do much with Ryder's work situation. We've sort of put it on hold while he deals with some work issues."

"Your dad must love that," Tatiana said. "Or has he come around to liking your fiancé?"

"He hasn't. You don't think my dad would make a labor complaint against Ryder's company, do you?" she asked her friend. "I know he really felt like Ryder had some part in that financial investigation he was under."

"I don't know what your dad would do. But those two men don't get along. Maybe you should take this time while he's working so much to think about whether you two can make this work," Tatiana said.

No. She didn't want to take a break from Ryder or their wedding. She loved him.

"Just think about it," Tatiana said. "I'd hate to see you get hurt."

"Okay," she said, ending the call a few minutes later.

She put her phone and her wine down on the table and walked to the window. She loved Ryder and she wasn't about to leave him. Was she? Was that the only way to give them some peace? Tatiana wasn't wrong when she said that her father and Ryder were never going to get along and she was tired of always being in the middle.

But leaving the man she loved wasn't a solution.

Angela's phone vibrated. Melinda had sent her a thank-you text with a funny gif of two spinsters sitting on a beach, talking about the good life and she sent back the laughing emoji, but she didn't want to be sitting on that beach with her twin. She wanted Ryder by her side. And maybe if she could find this Willem Inwood, she could talk to him and figure out if he knew her dad. Maybe if she could find a way to bridge the distance between the two men, she'd finally be able to enjoy being in love with the man of her dreams.

Two days later, Melinda was still faking it like a champ at work and with her social engagements. Slade hadn't called and she didn't expect him to. Alfie had glanced at her ring finger and lack of engagement ring and raised one eyebrow in question, but she'd just shaken her head and he'd let it lie. Late in the afternoon of the second day, she had a call from Henri, Philomena Conti's butler, asking if she had time to stop by for drinks with Mrs. Conti.

Melinda wanted to say no, not sure she was ready to talk to Slade's grandmother, but she knew that she'd just be putting off the inevitable. She needed to start getting closure with all of the people who connected her to Slade Bartelli. She had already decided to step down from the art council because she didn't want to accidentally run into him again. She would still fund the arts and had reached out to the Houston Museum of Fine Arts to see if they had any room on their board for her.

"Alfie, I'm going to be leaving in a few minutes. Do you mind letting the building security team know, so they can make sure no one is waiting for me?" she asked.

"Not a problem, boss lady. My boyfriend and I are having a few friends over for dinner tonight and we'd love it if you'd come and join us."

"Oh, Alfie, thank you for the invite. I'd love to come over. Text me the time and what I can bring," she said, hugging her assistant.

This was good. She needed to be making more after-hours plans. Last night she'd spent sitting in front of the TV, watching *Pride and Prejudice* and eating a huge bag of potato chips. She really couldn't do that again. The pregnancy book she'd been reading warned that eating for two was an urban myth.

She grabbed her bag and straightened the jacket on her Chanel suit as she walked out of her office. She smiled at Alfie and reminded herself how lucky she'd been to build a life where she was surrounded by people who genuinely cared for her. She knew she was going to need those friends in the coming months.

She drove to Philomena's house and tried not to think about the last time she'd been there. Their lunch plans had fallen through and this was the first occasion she'd been back. So many emotions. She'd been excited and nervous to start the charade of being Slade's fiancée and then had found out he'd been pushed to meet her. That should have been a red flag, but she hadn't seen it that way. Not after he'd pulled her into his arms. But that was sex. And she was old enough to understand that sex didn't equal emotions.

She sighed as she pulled into the circle drive and got out of her car. Henri answered the door and led her into the sitting room, where Philomena was waiting for her.

"Thank you, Melinda, for dropping by on such short notice," Philomena said, standing up to give Melinda a hug and then stepping back and sitting in her armchair again. "What would you like to drink?"

"Just some ice water," Melinda said. "The heat today is intense."

"It is," Philomena agreed, gesturing for Melinda to take a seat, and when she did, she noticed the ring box on the table next to the older woman.

"I guess Slade has told you we aren't engaged anymore," Melinda said.

"He did," she said. "He told me he couldn't be the man you wanted him to be."

She sighed. Her stomach hurt a bit, probably

from the tension of having to make this sound palatable to his sweet grandmother. "Slade is…"

She had no idea how to say this and her stomach was starting to knot and hurt really bad. She put her hand over it and leaned forward, realizing that this was more than tension. The pain was intensifying and shooting through her. She moaned.

"Are you okay? You look really pale," Philomena said.

"My stomach," Melinda muttered, holding her hand over her belly and praying that there wasn't something wrong with the baby. She couldn't help herself; she started crying.

"Henri," Philomena called out to her butler, who appeared at the doorway. "Get the car. We need to take Melinda to the emergency room." Then she directed her calm eyes to Melinda. "It will be okay," she said.

"It might not be," Melinda said. She'd always been worried that her age could be a factor in the pregnancy. "I'm so sorry, Philomena."

"Darling girl, you're not the first person to get sick in my home," she said. "And you mean more to me than any of them."

"You're very sweet, but Slade and I were lying to you. I need you to know that we didn't mean any harm." She could hardly speak. The pain was sharp now and she had to breathe heavily through it.

She didn't want to lose her baby, she realized.

She had just started getting used to the idea of being a mother. She wanted this child.

"I know it was meant to be a temporary engagement," Philomena said. "Slade told me when he brought the ring back. He also told me that you objected to it, but he'd insisted and that the reason you broke it off was his fault."

She shouldn't have been surprised Slade had taken all of the blame. He was always trying to protect her. "There's more to it than that. We—" She groaned as another sharp pain ripped through her. "I think I need to go. My stomach…"

She stood up and she stumbled, almost falling, but Philomena was there to hold her. "Henri. We need to get Melinda to the hospital now."

Philomena held her hand as Henri rushed them to the hospital. Philomena took care of everything and stayed by Melinda's side, only stepping outside the cubicle when the nurse came, and Melinda felt alone and scared.

She told the nurse that she was pregnant and was having stomach pains, and she couldn't stop crying and feeling so very alone.

"Want me to get your grandma back in here?" the nurse asked.

"She's not my family," Melinda said, realizing how sad that made her. "Will you ask her to text my sister and Slade?"

"I will," the nurse said. "The doctor will be in here in a moment."

The nurse walked away and Melinda lay there on the hospital bed, staring at the ceiling and praying for her baby. She felt the tears streaming down her face. She felt scared and alone, and as much as she told herself not to, she wished Slade were here with her.

Fourteen

Nonna's call had come just as Slade was finishing up a meeting with his father. His head pounded and his heart raced when he heard Melinda was in the hospital. He wasted no time, turning from his father and running for the door. He'd had a lot of time to think about everything that Melinda had said, and living without her even for a few days had left him questioning his choices. He couldn't bear the thought of losing her now.

"I have to go, Dad. Something's wrong with Melinda."

"I'll drive," his father said, coming up behind him. "Do you remember when your mom cut her hand with that knife when you were about seven?"

He nodded. Why was his dad bringing that up now?

"I freaked out and barely was able to get us to the emergency room for them to take care of it. When the woman you love is in pain, it messes with your head."

"Yeah, it does," he said to his father. And to be honest, Slade was panicking. He wasn't sure how he thought that loving Melinda and living apart from her was going to work out, but he knew now that he wanted to be by her side and that he'd never again let anything keep them apart.

In their hours-long conversation, his father had reassured him that he didn't have to worry about the family coming after him. But the most startling thing his father told him was that he'd been working with local law enforcement for the last few years, trying to go clean. And he'd spent that time hoping that he'd be able to rebuild his relationship with Slade.

The sense of relief that had flooded him drove home how big of a weight the worry of bringing Melinda and their baby into a world where his father was still a crime boss had been on him. He'd always thought that he was cool with the rumors and whispered comments behind his back or at the very least, that he'd learned to deal with them, but he knew now he hadn't been.

His dad was changing, trying hard to make a new life for himself, and he hoped to forge a relationship with him. Slade knew he could change too.

Be the man that Melinda needed him to be.

It wasn't going to be easy, but she was worth the effort. He was going to have to work hard to convince her to give him another chance. To show her that he wanted her as his wife because, as his father had said, loving a woman wasn't easy but it was the best damned thing a man could experience.

He wanted that. He wanted to raise his child with Melinda, not watch from the distance. He could protect them. He deserved the happy family and the life he could have with Melinda. The one that he'd always been afraid to let himself want.

Carlo dropped him off at the entrance to the emergency room and Slade ran into the waiting area. Nonna and Henri were sitting off to one side. He went to see his grandmother. "Where's Melinda? Any word?"

"Room three," Nonna said, shaking her head. "I've got a call into the head of the hospital board to see if he can get her seen sooner."

"Thanks, Nonna," he said, rushing to room three. He opened the door and stepped inside and his heart broke.

Melinda looked so small, lying on the hospital bed. Her head was back and tears were rolling down her face. Had she lost the baby?

"Baby cakes, I'm here," he said.

He took her hand in his and when she looked up at him, he knew that he'd never leave her again. He couldn't. They belonged together.

"I'm sorry. I love you and I want to be the man you deserve," he said.

"You might not need to be," she said on a sob. "I don't know what's going on but I'm having horrible stomach pain. I think something's wrong with our baby."

"Don't worry. I'm here with you and I've got you," he told her. "Whatever it is, we'll face it together."

The doctor and nurse came back in and examined Melinda. All Slade could do was stand by her side, holding her hand because when he'd dropped it and moved away, she reached out to him. He tried to project a calm appearance but inside he was freaking out. This baby that he'd been unsure of was the reason why he'd been able to finally figure out what was important in his life.

And he realized that he didn't want anything to happen to Melinda or the child. He needed them both. They were the grounding he'd been so afraid to find. He thought they would tie him to a future that would be complicated and hard, but he realized now that without Melinda by his side nothing else mattered.

He looked up as the doctor spoke. "I'm going to have some tests run, but there is no bleeding, so I think your baby is okay. The pain could be from bloating or gas. Once I have the results of your tests, I'll be able to confirm it."

The doctor left and the nurse had Melinda transferred to a wheelchair and took her for the tests. He walked beside her, holding her hand tightly, squeezing it gently.

"If you want to go into the waiting room," the nurse said to him, "I'll come and get you when she's back."

He nodded and followed them out to the hallway, just watching as Melinda was wheeled away. He'd never felt like someone was his world before this moment. Had never allowed himself to care this deeply for another person or to hope that one day he'd have a family of his own. And he was so close to having it; he didn't want to lose it now. Slade was alone in the hallway when someone touched his shoulder. He glanced around to see his father standing there.

"I know we have a long way to go, son," Carlo said. "But I wanted you to know that I'm here. You are the only family that matters to me. Philomena is waiting to talk to you, and I think Melinda's family is here, so I'll go out the back, but I needed to see you."

"Thanks, Dad," Slade said. He and his father still had a ways to go before they would have a real relationship, but they were working on it. Slade hugged his father and then he left, going down the hallway away from the waiting room.

Slade stepped into the waiting room where Angela had joined Nonna. They both looked over at him expectantly.

"She's having some tests done, but the doctor thinks the baby's okay. We'll know more when she gets back. He said it could be gas. I'm praying that it is."

"We all are," Angela said. "Can we wait in her room? I want to see her when she gets back."

"The nurse said she'd come and get us," Slade said, sitting down in the chair and putting his head in his hands. He had never felt so powerless before. He didn't often pray; it wasn't something that made much sense to him since he was a man who made things happen by taking action. But in this moment, he reached out to God or the universe… anyone who was listening.

"Please protect my family," he said. Knowing in his heart that he needed them more than anything else.

As soon as Melinda was back in her cubicle in the emergency room, Angela rushed in to see her. Her twin hugged her and sat on the bed next to her. "Are you okay?"

"I think so. The doctor thinks it might be just regular stomach pain and nothing to do with the baby. We should know something soon. How embarrassing if it turns out to just be gas," Melinda said.

"Not embarrassing at all. It was probably stress. I hope that it is just that, so we don't have to worry anymore. Slade is beside himself. He wanted to come in, but then wasn't sure if you wanted to see him. I've never seen Slade Bartelli acting the way he is right now," Angela said.

"I know. I think he's worried about the baby." And her, Melinda wanted to add. But she needed to be cautious. She had promised herself to stop seeing Slade as she wanted him to be and to only see the man he really was.

His grandmother was out there, and she had to wonder if he was playing the concerned boyfriend for her. But the way he'd held her hand, the things he'd said to her before… Maybe it had been the pain making her see it in a different way, but she thought that Slade was being genuine. He'd never been one to pretend to feel something he didn't. It had only been her perception that she didn't trust.

"I think he's worried about you," Angela said. "I heard him talking to his grandmother and she was comforting him. Telling him that he'd have time to fix this."

"This?"

"Well, obviously I don't know what they were talking about, but I'm pretty sure she meant things with you. I had my doubts about him. He seemed like a bit of fun and you definitely were overdue for some fun, but now I think he might be the real deal, Mels."

She hoped her sister was right.

Angela stayed until the doctor came in and gave her the test results and the all clear. Her sister left to allow Melinda to get changed into her street clothes and to go fill the prescription the doctor gave her, but only after promising to send Slade in.

Melinda wanted to talk to him privately before she went out to see Philomena. She hoped that none of the society bloggers had been alerted to her being at the hospital. She wasn't ready for all of Houston society to know that she was pregnant until she knew what was happening between her and Slade.

Someone knocked on the door and she called out for them to come in. It was Slade. He looked haggard, as if he'd been running his hands through his hair, but he smiled when he saw her.

"You're okay?" he asked.

"Yes. Just some stomach problems and the doctor has given me some medicine to take. He also wants me to try a bland diet for a few days to make sure that it's not serious. I'm supposed to go and see my doctor tomorrow."

"Thank God," he said. "I was so worried about you."

"I was worried too," she admitted. "So why are you here?"

"I guess that's a fair question," he said. "I want you to know that the last three days have been the longest of my life. I thought I was protecting you by leaving and for the first night while I drank a bottle of Jack in my den, I almost believed it. But the next morning I realized that you had been right when you said I wasn't eighteen anymore. I'd been afraid to reach out to my father because I knew that I had wanted that relationship to be something it couldn't be."

"Fair enough," she said. "Hopefully now you can resolve that."

She still wasn't sure why he was here. He'd been pretty adamant that he didn't want to be a family man.

"I already did. Once I realized that I needed you back in my life, I realized I had to talk to Dad and let him know that I wanted no part of his life," Slade said.

"Good. What did he say?" she asked. Slade was always going to have a big gaping hole inside of him until he resolved his issues with his dad.

"He got it. We aren't totally there yet, but we're working toward it. He drove me here today."

"He did?" she asked, surprised.

"Yes. He said when the woman I loved was in danger, I shouldn't be driving," Slade said.

Love.

"You know you don't have to say you love me," she said. She wanted those words to be true, but she was afraid of them as well.

"I know I don't. You also know I don't lie, baby cakes. It might take you a while to believe them and that's okay," he said. "Because I'm not going anywhere. I'm going to stay by your side for the rest of our lives and tell you every day how much I love you."

He came over to her and took her hand in his, and then got down on his knee in front of her. "I know that I don't deserve you and for so long I was afraid I couldn't be the man you deserved, but I promise you that I will try to be. I love you, Melinda Perry. Please, will you consider marrying me? Not for the media or because your dad will likely kick my butt when he finds out you're pregnant, but because I love you and can't imagine my life without you by my side as my wife."

She looked down at him kneeling on the hospital floor and looking up at her with love in his eyes and hope on his face.

"Yes, Slade. Yes, I will," she said, tugging him to his feet. And he pulled her into his arms, kissing her deeply.

She pulled back, smiling up at him. "This whole thing started with a kiss."

"Good. I like kissing you and we can do it often to remind us of how we got our start."

The engagement party at Philomena Conti's house on the last Saturday in September was spectacular and the society bloggers who were streaming live from the event were saying it was the party of the year. Angela stood in the corner, watching

Melinda and Slade and feeling more than a tiny bit envious. Ryder had canceled on her at the last moment, so she was there alone. Her father was more than happy that she had come without Ryder and had told her more than once. But then her father was in a good mood and had maybe had one too many Lone Star beers. He was toasting Melinda, and Angela loved seeing her twin so happy.

She glowed with a look that Angela thought only someone in love had. Slade was completely doting on her twin, which both Melinda and Angela thought was funny. He had moved his office into Melinda's condo and had been working from home until the doctor gave her the all clear to go back to work.

"She looks happy," Tatiana said, coming over to Angela and handing her a glass of champagne.

"She does," Angela said.

"Soon that will be you," Tatiana said. "Where is your fiancé?"

She wasn't so sure. Ryder had been more distant than ever. "He had to work."

"He's been working a lot of hours lately. I hope you aren't marrying a workaholic."

"There are just a few things going on that are taking more attention than Ryder usually has to give them," she said.

"Probably for the best he isn't here, given how much your father and he don't get along," Tatiana said. "And this is Melinda's day."

"It is," she said, grateful when Melinda waved her over to her side. Lately, Tatiana hadn't seemed as supportive of her relationship with Ryder. She wondered if her best friend saw something that Angela herself was missing.

She hugged Melinda as soon as she got to her side.

"Where's Ryder?" Melinda asked.

"Oh, he couldn't be here. He had to work," Angela said.

"Dang it. I wanted to get a picture of the four of us together. Maybe we could have dinner next week. Just the four of us. Now that my engagement is for real, maybe we can seriously think about a double wedding," Melinda said.

"Let's have dinner and discuss it," Angela said. But with Ryder refusing to discuss a date, she doubted he was going to be all gung ho for a double wedding. She stayed for another hour and then made her excuses to head home.

When she got to her condo, Ryder was waiting in the living room for her. She was so happy to see him, she didn't think anything of it when he said, "Hey, sorry to do this today, but I think we need to talk."

"Okay," she said, sitting down beside him on the sofa. "How did you know when I'd be home?"

"Find My Friends app," he said.

"Oh. What's up? Melinda is crazy happy and in love with Slade. She brought up a double wedding—"

"Let me stop you there."

Her heart sunk and she felt a knot in the pit of her stomach. "Why?"

"Because I know that you're torn between me and your vengeful father. I can't ask you to choose between me and your family."

"But you're not asking me to do that," she said, her chest constricting. She didn't want to break up with him. She loved Ryder. And even though it wasn't easy to deal with her father, she still hoped someday her dad would come around and see Ryder the way she did.

"I know, but I can't bear to see you destroyed because of me. I love you too much, Angela. I think it's best if we end this now," he said, holding out his hand.

She blinked, trying not to cry. He couldn't really mean this. "We can make it work."

"Not without destroying your family and mine," he said. "I'm afraid my mind is made up."

She took the engagement ring off her finger and dropped it into the palm of his hand, starting to cry as he turned and walked out the door. As soon as it closed, she collapsed on the couch. Her heart was breaking in two. How was she going to live without the man she loved?

She missed her mom. She needed her mom. She would have called Melinda, but she didn't want to ruin her twin's day. She grabbed a tub of Blue Bell's Mardi Gras King Cake ice cream and opened up the digital file of her mom's memorial service. She sighed as, through her tears, she watched everyone celebrate her mom's life. In the video, Tatiana was by her side the entire time. She really was a good friend and Angela was lucky to have her. Melinda looked so lost and broken. Angela was glad her sister had found Slade Bartelli. His love had helped Melinda find new purpose.

She saw someone in the corner of the video frame. A young man. Who was that?

She rewound it and then hit Pause and gasped as she realized who it was.

Tatiana's half brother...Willem Inwood.

Tatiana hated him and his mother, but why wouldn't she have said that he was her brother when Angela had asked? Was it because she didn't want to bring up her family drama?

She thought about calling Ryder and telling him, but she didn't think she could bear to hear his voice.

Slade carried Melinda over the threshold into her bedroom later that evening. This had been the best day of her life. The one that she'd been secretly hoping for since Slade has asked her out that first time. She had been afraid to hope that a love like this would come into her life. The only wrinkle had been the fact that Angela's fiancé hadn't been there. She was so happy and in love, and for this one moment it seemed her entire family was in a good place.

She had her arms wrapped around Slade's shoulders and only had eyes for him. He put her on her feet next to the bed.

Leaning down, he kissed her so lovingly before he began undressing her. He traced a path down her body and around her breasts once she was naked. Then his fingers danced over her belly as he went down on his knees next to her and kissed her stomach. "Hello, baby. We can't wait to meet you."

She caught her breath, tangling her fingers in his hair. Slade, as always, once he committed himself to something or in this case, her, he was 100 percent on board.

"I love you, Slade."

"I love you too, baby cakes."

He lifted her off her feet, placed her in the center of the bed and made love to her. Then he held her in his arms as they planned for their future, and for the first time in her life, she felt like her real world and the world she was always making in her head were one.

Epilogue

Well, that didn't go the way I'd hoped. Sterling hasn't been arrested for the murder and Angela and Ryder still care for each other. Perry is proud as punch that Melinda is getting married and giving him a grandchild.

Damn.

I hate this. Dreams of the man that I accidentally killed aren't making it any easier to move past the guilt. If the cops would just arrest and charge someone—preferably Sterling Perry—with the murder, maybe I could move on.

And then there's Melinda. Seeing her so happy and pregnant stirs so many emotions. It can't be

*jealousy because no one would ever be envious of
a goody-goody like Melinda Perry.*

*But there's a part of me that is. What is it about
the Perry family that they always get what they
want, while my own life keeps spiraling out of control? The plans that I have been working on for so
long are slowly slipping out of my control.*

*Maybe involving Willem was a mistake. But he
was keen to make sure that Ryder Currin and Sterling Perry pay for what they have done to us. But
he's never been smart. Not smart enough to do
something simple without leaving his fingerprints
all over it. But I'm not about to let Willem's screwup
be the end of the road. Whatever it takes I will bring
down Sterling Perry and Ryder Currin.*

* * * * *

COMING NEXT MONTH FROM

⬡ HARLEQUIN®
Desire

Available October 1, 2019

#2689 TANGLED WITH A TEXAN

Texas Cattleman's Club: Houston • by Yvonne Lindsay

From the first, wealthy rancher Cord Galicia and Detective Zoe Warren create sparks. She's in town to question Cord's friend and neighbor, and he'll have none of it. So he seduces her as a distraction. But his plan is about to backfire...

#2690 BOMBSHELL FOR THE BLACK SHEEP

Southern Secrets • by Janice Maynard

Black sheep heir Hartley Tarleton is back in Charleston to deal with his family's scandals. But a one-night stand with artist Fiona James leads to a little scandal of his own. How will he handle fatherhood—and his irresistible desire for this woman?

#2691 CHRISTMAS SEDUCTION

The Bachelor Pact • by Jessica Lemmon

When Tate Duncan learns his life is a lie, he asks Hayden Green to pose as his fiancée to meet his newfound birth parents. But when real passion takes over, Hayden wonders if it's all just holiday fantasy, or a gift that runs much deeper.

#2692 READY FOR THE RANCHER

Sin City Secrets • by Zuri Day

Rich rancher and CEO Adam Breedlove is all business. But when a chance encounter reconnects him with his best friend's sister, their forbidden chemistry spells trouble. And when their business interests get entangled, the stakes get even higher...

#2693 ONE NIGHT WITH HIS EX

One Night • by Katherine Garbera

Hooking up with an ex is *always* a bad idea. But when it comes to Hadley Everton, Mauricio Velasquez throws reason out the window. The morning after, is past betrayal still too steep a hurdle, or are these exes back on?

#2694 SEDUCTIVE SECRETS

Sweet Tea and Scandal • by Cat Schield

Security entrepreneur Paul Watts knows deception, so when a beautiful stranger charms his hospitalized grandfather, Paul smells trouble. Lia Marsh seems too good to be true. So good, he falls for her himself! Now her secrets could tear them apart—or bind them even closer.

YOU CAN FIND MORE INFORMATION ON UPCOMING HARLEQUIN® TITLES, FREE EXCERPTS AND MORE AT WWW.HARLEQUIN.COM.

HDCNM0919

Get 4 **FREE REWARDS!**

We'll send you 2 FREE Books <u>plus</u> 2 FREE Mystery Gifts.

Harlequin® Desire books feature heroes who have it all: wealth, status, incredible good looks... everything but the right woman.

FREE Value Over **$20**

YES! Please send me 2 FREE Harlequin® Desire novels and my 2 FREE gifts (gifts are worth about $10 retail). After receiving them, if I don't wish to receive any more books, I can return the shipping statement marked "cancel." If I don't cancel, I will receive 6 brand-new novels every month and be billed just $4.55 per book in the U.S. or $5.24 per book in Canada. That's a savings of at least 13% off the cover price! It's quite a bargain! Shipping and handling is just 50¢ per book in the U.S. and $1.25 per book in Canada.* I understand that accepting the 2 free books and gifts places me under no obligation to buy anything. I can always return a shipment and cancel at any time. The free books and gifts are mine to keep no matter what I decide.

225/326 HDN GNND

Name (please print)

Address   Apt. #

City   State/Province   Zip/Postal Code

Mail to the **Reader Service:**
IN U.S.A.: P.O. Box 1341, Buffalo, NY 14240-8531
IN CANADA: P.O. Box 603, Fort Erie, Ontario L2A 5X3

Want to try 2 free books from another series! Call 1-800-873-8635 or visit www.ReaderService.com.

---

*Developer Tate Duncan has a family he never knew,
and only the sympathy and sexiness of yoga instructor
Hayden Green offers escape. So he entices her into
spending Christmas with him as he meets his birth
parents...posing as his fiancée! But when they give in to
dangerously real attraction, their ruse—and the secrets
they've been keeping—could implode!*

Read on for a sneak peek of
Christmas Seduction
by Jessica Lemmon.

"I don't believe you want to talk about yoga." She lifted
dark, inquisitive eyebrows. "You look like you have
something interesting to talk about."

The pull toward her was real and raw—the realest thing
he'd felt in a while.

"I didn't plan on talking about it..." he admitted, but she
must have heard the ellipsis at the end of that sentence.

She tilted her head, a sage interested in whatever he
said next. Wavy dark brown hair surrounded a cherubic
heart-shaped face, her deep brown eyes at once tender
and inviting. How had he not noticed before? She was
alarmingly beautiful.

"I'm sorry." Her palm landed on his forearm. "I'm
prying. You don't have to say anything."

"There are aspects of my life I was certain of a month
and a half ago," he said, idly stroking her hand with his

thumb. "I was certain that my parents' names were William and Marion Duncan." He offered a sad smile as Hayden's eyebrows dipped in confusion. "I suppose they technically still are my parents, but they're also not. I'm adopted."

Her plush mouth pulled into a soft frown, but she didn't interrupt.

"I recently learned that the agency—" or more accurately, the kidnappers "—lied about my birth parents. Turns out they're alive. And I have a brother." He paused before clarifying, "A twin brother."

Hayden's lashes fluttered. "Wow."

"Fraternal, but he's a good-looking bastard. I just need… I need…" Dropping his head in his hands, he trailed off, muttering to the floor, "Christ, I have no idea what I need."

He felt the couch shift and dip, and then Hayden's hand was on his back, moving in comforting circles.

"I've had my share of family drama, trust me. But nothing like what you're going through. It's okay for you to feel unsure. Lost."

He faced her. This close, he could smell her soft lavender perfume and see the gold flecks in her dark eyes. He hadn't planned on coming here, or on sitting on her couch and spilling his heart out. He and Hayden were friendly, not friends. But her comforting touch on his back, the way her words seemed to soothe the recently broken part of him…

Maybe what Tate needed was her.

What will happen when Tate brings Hayden home for Christmas?

Find out in Christmas Seduction *by Jessica Lemmon. Available October 2019 wherever Harlequin® Desire books and ebooks are sold.*

www.Harlequin.com

Want to give in to temptation with steamy tales of irresistible desire?

Check out **Harlequin® Presents®, Harlequin® Desire** and **Harlequin® Kimani™ Romance** books!

New books available every month!

CONNECT WITH US AT:

Facebook.com/groups/HarlequinConnection

 Facebook.com/HarlequinBooks

 Twitter.com/HarlequinBooks

 Instagram.com/HarlequinBooks

 Pinterest.com/HarlequinBooks

ReaderService.com

**ROMANCE WHEN
YOU NEED IT**

PGENRE2018

Love Harlequin romance?

DISCOVER.

Be the first to find out about promotions, news and exclusive content!

Facebook.com/HarlequinBooks

Twitter.com/HarlequinBooks

Instagram.com/HarlequinBooks

Pinterest.com/HarlequinBooks

ReaderService.com

EXPLORE.

Sign up for the Harlequin e-newsletter and download a free book from any series at **TryHarlequin.com.**

CONNECT.

Join our Harlequin community to share your thoughts and connect with other romance readers!
Facebook.com/groups/HarlequinConnection

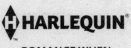

H HARLEQUIN®

**ROMANCE WHEN
YOU NEED IT**

HSOCIAL2018

THE WORLD IS BETTER WITH

Romance

Harlequin has everything from contemporary, passionate and heartwarming to suspenseful and inspirational stories.

Whatever your mood, we have a romance just for you!

Connect with us to find your next great read, special offers and more.

f /HarlequinBooks

🐦 @HarlequinBooks

www.HarlequinBlog.com

www.Harlequin.com/Newsletters

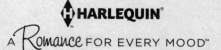

HARLEQUIN®

A *Romance* FOR EVERY MOOD™

www.Harlequin.com

SERIESHALOAD2015